Betty King is married and lives in Hertfordshire. She suspects she inherited her desire to write about the past from an ancestor, Thomas Martin of Norfolk. An antiquarian of some note, he once possessed an extensive collection of ancient manuscripts containing the original Paston Letters, and he published several works including a History of Thetford.

MARGARET OF ANJOU

Margaret of Anjou, closely related to the throne of France, was a glittering prize in the marriage lottery of the fifteenth century. When the statesmen of England sought her hand for Henry VI they saw in such a union a permanent solution to the Hundred Years war. Sadly, Margaret was soon to discover that her husband was more suitable for a monastic life than a wedded one. Her passionate nature, so woefully neglected, led her deeper and deeper into trouble, and she was prevented by her high destiny from enjoying the society of the man she loved.

Books by Betty King
Published by The House of Ulverscroft:

WE ARE TOMORROW'S PAST
THE FRENCH COUNTESS
THE ROSE BOTH RED AND WHITE

BETTY KING

MARGARET OF ANJOU

Complete and Unabridged

ULVERSCROFT
Leicester

First published in Great Britain in 1974 by
Robert Hale Limited
London

First Large Print Edition
published 2000
by arrangement with
Robert Hale Limited
London

British Library CIP Data

King, Betty, *1919* –
    Margaret of Anjou.—Large print ed.—
Ulverscroft large print series: romance
1. Love stories
2. Large type books
I. Title
823.9'14 [F]

ISBN 0–7089–4231–8

Published by
F. A. Thorpe (Publishing)
Anstey, Leicestershire

Set by Words & Graphics Ltd.
Anstey, Leicestershire
Printed and bound in Great Britain by
T. J. International Ltd., Padstow, Cornwall

This book is printed on acid-free paper

For Mme la Marquise de Dreux Brézé

and

M. et Mme le Comte et
Comtesse de Colbert
of the Chateau de Brézé near Saumur

as a small token of my gratitude for their
great kindness in welcoming me
to their home and enabling me to see
where Pierre de Brézé once lived.

Acknowledgments

My grateful thanks are expressed to the Staff of the London Library, the Staff of the Library of the Borough of Enfield, the Staff of the British Museum Reading Room and the Chief Librarian of the Library of Bergerac, France, Mademoiselle Petit, for their help in finding me the sources of this book: and to Susan Fane who provided me with an excellent and most useful chronological table. I am especially indebted to my husband for his loving support and continuing encouragement.

Bibliography

The End of the House of Lancaster
  R. Storey, 1966.
The Wars of the Roses
  J. R. Lander, 1965.
Warwick the Kingmaker
  P. M. Kendall, 1957.
The Life and Times of Margaret of Anjou
  Mrs. Hookham, 1872.
The Paston Letters, Edited
  James Gairdner, 1904.
Margaret of Anjou Queen of England
  J. J. Bagley, 1948.
The Fifteenth Century
  E. F. Jacob, 1961.
Letters of Queen Margaret of Anjou
  Ed. C. Monro, 1863.
The Dictionary of National Biography
Louis XI
  P. M. Kendall, 1971.

1

'To be a queen in bondage is more vile
Than is a slave in base servility;
For princes should be free.'

Henry VI, Shakespeare

Margaret leant against the stone of the embrasure revelling in the May sunshine which penetrated her bones and lulled her into a most pleasant sensation of well-being. She had come to the small room which her father used as an atelier in a restless fit of discontentment that had made her weary of the chatter in the women's solar. For some time there had been an atmosphere in the castle of Angers hitherto associated with the feasts of Christmas or her name day; an excitement more baffling since it seemed to include Margaret yet shut her out. She wished, for the hundredth time, that her father, René, Duke of Anjou and King of Naples would return from Tours where he was attending the court of Charles VII. René's company for an hour was more satisfying than an afternoon of useless

1

conversation about the shape of headwear favoured by the ladies of the French court; a topic which seemed of vital interest to the women attending her mother, Isabella. Not that Margaret disliked fashion or pretty gowns but she found more satisfaction in wearing a becoming dress and catching the admiring glances it evoked than in a tedious discussion about the merits of gauze or silk veils.

René would have sensed his daughter's disquiet and would have encouraged her to finish the drawing she was making for a new stained glass window in the castle chapel. It should have been simple to slide down from the window seat, where the warm scent of early roses drifted, and start the task without him but the place was dead when he was absent and it was almost more than she could do to look at the stacks of wooden panels leaning against the walls. Each of the paintings, complete or in the process of completion, was a projection of René's warm and interesting personality.

It was not difficult for Margaret to find a reason for her own restiveness for she was always like this when her father was away from home; a distinct legacy from the terrible times when he had been a prisoner of the Duke of Burgundy. During those five years

Isabella, brave and independent as she undoubtedly was, had been hard-pressed to fill the position of two parents and Margaret had suffered more than her brother or elder sister. It was being the baby of the family and spoilt that accounted for this, as Margaret had overheard from her mother's waiting women more times than she cared to count, because it was René who was the idol of her childhood and now a lodestar and a companion who encouraged her artistic ability.

Margaret sighed and looked down into the walled courtyard below, empty except for a woman carrying a wicker basket of clean linen on her head. If only Louis, her father's page, was somewhere in the castle it would be fun to seek him out and climb to the battlements to watch the river. Several times they had exchanged glances and once during a dance in the great hall they had held hands; it would relieve the tedium considerably to lean close to him and indulge in the delicious danger of tempting him to kiss her. Holy Mary, Margaret found herself praying, at least when my father and his advisers decide which of my suitors I am to marry let him be a man lusty in bed as well as a master in his own dukedom.

She was stopped in her daydreams by the

sound of a thin, distant horn and leapt down from the stone seat with the feline grace of a sun-soaked cat. Her father was coming home and life could begin again.

René and his daughter met in the courtyard, his haste to be among his family as great as Margaret's to have him home. The Duke of Anjou at this time was a man of thirty-six years, of medium height but well built. His thinning hair was brown-gold and his complexion fairer than most of his compatriots; his grey eyes were humorous and his mouth turned upward ready for the smile which was never far distant. Brother-in-law of Charles VII of France he had inherited the kingdom of Naples and Sicily together with the duchies of Anjou and Bar. His wife Isabella of Lorraine, who had married him when he was twelve and she ten, had borne him four children and had shown the nature of her courage during his captivity when she had stormed across France, taking two of her offspring with her, to subjugate René's distant Neapolitan possession. Not quite as widely read or as artistic as her husband she had insisted that Margaret should be educated to a high standard and when she considered her own knowledge to fall short of this requirement had put her youngest child to share the tutoring of Antoine de Salle with her elder brothers.

René's marriage with Isabella, which had been proposed as a gesture of peace in the constant internecine wars waged between the French principalities, worsened the situation rather than smoothed the problems and had resulted in René's falling foul of the new Duke of Burgundy when his uncle, the old Duke, was murdered by the forces of Charles of France. For five weary years René had paid the price of this displeasure by captivity and had eventually bought his release with an enormous ransom and the promise that his elder daughter Yolande should marry Burgundy's son.

From this imprisonment René had hurried to the aid of his wife in Naples but eventually had had to concede defeat to a rival contestant and retire to Anjou to administer his remaining estates and play some part in the administration of Charles' kingdom.

It was from this last duty that he now came carrying a proposal of such magnitude that, with all his knowledge of the past, still left him somewhat dazed. He regarded his youngest child more searchingly than usual as she proffered her cheek for his kiss and suffered a pang of resentment that his pleasure in her was to be so swiftly curtailed.

Margaret, two months past her fourteenth birthday, was an almost exact counterpart of her mother at the same age, possessing her vitality and good looks. She glowed with health which shone in the brightness of her eyes and the colour of her skin and her abundant hair gleamed with much brushing and copper lights. Her voice was warm and inclined to be husky and she used her hands often to emphasize and illustrate her conversation; she was a young woman who would grace any man's table. Yet René prayed that the proposal which he had brought to Angers would meet with the approval of this mettlesome and attractive young woman; it was not often that Margaret displayed the temper which she had learnt early to control but there had been occasions when unfortunate grooms had felt the cut of her tongue as she had berated them for mismanaging one of her favourite ponies. Her future spouse had better be a firm disciplinarian or he might rue the day that he had taken Margaret of Anjou as consort.

If René saw questions in the eyes of his daughter he chose to ignore them and spoke of the very fine paper which he had purchased for her in Tours. 'You have never seen such quality, chicken; it's made in Augsburg and is infinitely superior to any which we have had from Italy in the past. It should do justice to those pigments Antoine managed to secure for you and I shall expect great results from the combination. Where is your mother?'

'In the solar,' Margaret replied with a sigh which was not lost on René.

'Well then, we'll seek her out together,' her father said and putting his arm about her shoulders went into the dim stairway; he would have to wait to tell Isabella the momentous news which he brought from Tours.

Not until the supper boards had been cleared and minstrels played for dancing was René able to speak freely with his wife and he had the uneasy suspicion that Margaret was fey and knew perfectly well that he brought tidings of her future which he was reluctant to impart to her. It was only his suggestion that his handsome young page should lead her out to dance which took Margaret from his side.

'Dearest,' René said in a hurried undertone, 'I have tried many times since my arrival to speak with you but it seemed impossible to find an opportunity. Has anyone spoken to Margaret about the real object of my visit to the King?'

'Of course not, René, surely you know me

better than that?' Isabella asked, a slight blush colouring her unwrinkled neck.

'I know you very well,' René said with a chuckle, 'and in every other matter but Margaret's marriage I should be prepared to lay down my life that you would keep your counsel.'

'On that matter also!' Isabella cried.

'Then who besides ourselves is privy to the question?'

'None but her nurse and my chief dame of the bed-chamber; I am quite certain that neither of them has breathed a word of Charles' plan.' Isabella turned to René. 'But do not bandy words with me now, tell me what has befallen. Has Suffolk really brought an offer of marriage from England?'

'He has indeed.'

'And you are not happy about it?'

'I feel as if I am giving my daughter as a sacrifice to a man who may be a monster for all I know. His father had one ambition in life and went a long way to bringing France to her knees in the pursuit of fulfilling his destiny; how do I know that his son is not like minded?'

'But surely this marriage is to seal the truce between France, Anjou and England? My dear, we are not so wealthy or so well endowed with worldly prosperity that we can afford to flout this offer for Margaret's hand.'

'You honestly feel in your heart that we should accept?'

'I do.'

René did not reply for a space but sat still, watching his daughter performing the intricate steps of a country dance; his page was accompanying her and her face was a study of innocent happiness as she smiled up at him. It seemed a pity to spoil such enjoyment with the heavy news he could not indefinitely postpone breaking to her.

'Very well, but I shall return to Tours alone tomorrow so that I may acquaint Charles, Suffolk and Orleans with our decision and ask you to bring Margaret to join me in a day or two. Only one thing I implore you and that is to leave me to tell her that we have accepted on her behalf; she may find it easier to bear away from here and with both of us to sustain her.'

'I am sure you are wise — and have I your permission to have some finery made for her?'

'She must have the best that Angers can provide. Find silks and lace and we'll think about the cost when she has left us.'

★ ★ ★

When Margaret heard that she and Isabella were to join René in Tours she did not need her mother to tell her that she was going there to be betrothed. It was, however, impossible to prise anything from her mother, and Margaret had to content herself with recalling the numerous suitors who had sought her hand in the past. Surely it could not be Burgundy's nephew, Charles of Nevers? Charles had almost married two women before his betrothal to Margaret had been suggested but he had eagerly enough thrown them aside for René's daughter. Nor had it been Charles who had broken off the negotiations but René himself who had stipulated that Margaret's children should inherit large portions of Sicily, Provence and Bar to the detriment of her sister, Yolande, who had been married off to yet another of Burgundy's nephews as part of René's ransom to that irascible old Duke. Surely it was not possible that René had now retracted and given his consent to this unlikely match?

Knowing her father as she did Margaret could not imagine that this might be the case, for if René could be accused of being a dilettante and a dreamer it could never be said that he went back on his word. Yet the new marriage proposal seemed to be of such importance that Margaret was being equipped with a trousseau that would have graced a Queen of France and no manner of pleading would elicit a grain of information from Isabella. Margaret was forced to accept defeat and possess herself with some measure of patience.

★　★　★

The day she and her mother set out from Angers was the best of the new summer with cloudless skies and the air heavy with the scent of roses and honeysuckle. Margaret enjoyed every moment of the departure in the crowded courtyard when the servants came to take farewell of their master's favourite daughter; she had a new dress for the occasion and received compliments on every side. It was surely a happy omen for the future, whatever news she was about to hear.

The large entourage, well-equipped with halberdiers, pikemen and knights carrying couched lances, took two days over the journey beside the Loire and spent the night at Saumur. This castle, perched on a rock, was surrounded by vineyards and had been built by Duke de Berry to the most magnificent design. René had often told Margaret that he had seen Books of the Hours in which Saumur had been depicted as the crown of artistic achievement and on this day, rising turret upon turret against an azure sky, it lived up to its reputation. Margaret had visited the castle before to pay her last respects to René's mother who had lived at Saumur during the period of her widowhood but she had never before recognized the striking beauty of the white stone towers surmounted with pointed roofs and pinnacles of beaten copper. For the short while that the chateau was spread out before her as she rode towards it Margaret felt a strange sense of elation that a building had never before aroused in her. When her party rode in under the gatehouse in sudden darkness she shivered and crossed herself in momentary panic. Was she indeed fey or was her inner excitement colouring her surroundings so that she seemed to be moving in a fairy tale world? She felt that she must curb her exuberance lest life, with its cruel disregard for personal happiness, might bring great disappointment to crush the mingled pride and hope that flowed about her. Perhaps, after all, it was only to Peter of Luxemborg that she was to be betrothed and all the fuss which had enthralled the household of Angers since René had departed for Tours was no more than a sop to soften the blow of a marriage which had been first proposed when she had been three years of age. Margaret felt it was well to keep some sense of proportion and by the time she had bathed and eaten the hearty dinner prepared for them by her grandmother's old chef she was light of heart and more than ready to join the company in dancing and singing; and if the handsome Louis partnered her more than once there could be no harm in that, for was she not already almost a married woman and able to allocate her favours as she chose?

In Tours she was disappointed to discover that she was not to be taken straight to Charles' residence but was to be lodged at the abbey of Beaumont-les-Tours with her mother. They had been but an hour in the pleasant rooms they were given when René came to join them.

He kissed his wife and Margaret, then held his daughter at arm's length to appraise her appearance. 'You look the picture of health,' he said. 'Your mother has told you why we have brought you here?'

'No!' cried mother and daughter vehemently together so that the three of them burst into laughter.

'My dear Isabella,' René said with a chuckle, looking from his wife's indignant face to Margaret's excited eyes and flushed cheeks, 'you have been as good as your word and kept your promise. Who said that a woman was incapable of keeping her counsel? But I should know that you, who were able to stand a seige of Naples on your own, are more than competent to respect my wishes.'

'But, father,' Margaret pleaded, exasperated, 'you speak only to mother and tell me nothing of what might be the most momentous happening of my life. Why have I been brought to Tours and to whom have you promised me?'

'My little cabbage, forgive me,' René said, all tenderness, 'I did not intend to slight you or keep you too long in suspense but the negotiations in which I have been involved with Charles and Orleans and the English Ambassador were more lengthy and more involved than I had imagined possible.'

'English Ambassador?' Margaret echoed, hardly able to believe her ears. 'You do not mean that you pledged me to marry some minor prince of England.' She felt light-headed and spoke as she might have done in a dream with a tongue suddenly wooden in her mouth. She knew very little more about France's northern neighbours than that England and her homeland were constantly at war and hated each other's ways like warring infidels. They lived, too, in draughty castles without proper means of heating to their rooms, drank beer and could hardly walk abroad for the constant rain and mists which beat upon them. Far, far better to marry Philip of Burgundy's nephew and live in abject subjugation than cross La Manche to cohabit with an uncultured boor who could neither read nor write and who thought more of the evil-smelling dogs crowding about his feet than the woman he married.

'If you want me to marry an Englishman,' she threatened in a voice several tones louder than she intended, 'I had rather become a nun.'

'My dear,' René soothed with maddening calm, 'do you really believe that your mother and I should give our precious daughter to some English squire?'

'Of course we should not!' Isabella interjected when Margaret seemed lost for words.

'Your mother is right, of course, as she so often is and I want to tell you that in accepting the offer of marriage of the King of England for you we are thinking not only of the future peace of his realms and our own but also of your future happiness, for Henry is a man of great culture — '

'You mean that I am going to become Queen of England?' Margaret said slowly, the colour fading from her cheeks and her trance-like condition deepening.

'Yes, that is exactly what we do mean and in half an hour from now the three of us will set out for Tours and we shall introduce you to the Earl of Suffolk and tell him how gladly you have received and accepted his lord's proposal. Come, sweeting, I knew very well that you would be shocked by the news that I had to tell but it is not a sentence of death I bring you.' René's tone was bracing and Margaret shook herself and managed to smile; she was glad that Isabella stood a little aside and busied herself selecting trinkets from a velvet covered box, for if her mother had made a move to comfort her she would have burst into tears. This was not the moment for the daughter of such parents to show signs of weakness. Margaret tilted her chin. 'Forgive me that I appear so stupid; for the moment I am somewhat overcome with the magnitude of the news you impart to me but it will soon pass, doubtless. But tell me, father, what is this King Henry? How has he heard of me and how can I come to love a man whose father hated France and thought of us all as his hereditary enemies? And did you not tell me that this very King whom you would have me wed was crowned King of France when he was only twelve in some ceremony in Notre Dame? How can we forget

16

all these past insults? What does our King think of my marrying a man who would usurp him any day of the week?'

'Well,' René said with a sharp intake of breath, 'that is all old history now and there is a strong faction — headed by the King of England himself and his chief adviser, his uncle Cardinal Beaufort — to have a lasting and enduring peace with France. My lord Suffolk, who is very much in King Henry's favour and confidence, will tell you that it is hoped that your marriage will consolidate their plans. By the time you leave for England — '

'That will not be for some time yet, I trust, so that you and my tutor Antoine can teach me more about this country which I shall have to adopt as my own.'

René hesitated long enough for his daughter to guess the reason for his diffidence. 'I am to go soon,' she stated in a flat, dull voice. 'Very well, you can rest assured that I shall not fail you. Tell me only one thing, is this King Henry young or old?'

Isabella and René exchanged glances. 'He is young, only twenty-three or four and very gentle and kindly by what his ambassador tells me. You musn't forget, Meg, that his mother was a French princess like yourself and when Katherine de Valois left her native

17

land after the battle of Agincourt to marry
Henry V she had a more difficult task than
that which confronts you now.'

'Is she still alive?' Margaret asked.

'She died about five years ago, I am told,'
René said and stooped to kiss his daughter.
'Come, put on the prettiest of your new
gowns and let me show these English
ambassadors how fortunate their country will
be to have you as their Queen.'

2

William de la Pole, Earl of Suffolk, great
Seneschal of the royal house of England and
Henry VI's ambassador in the matter of his
marriage with Margaret of Anjou, was, in the
May of 1444, at the height of his power and
full of hope for his future. An ambitious man
he had been prudent enough to ask from his
sovereign a written guarantee that he acted
with Henry's complete authority in coming to
France to seek the hand of René of Anjou's
talented and beautiful daughter. He had
considered this step vital for, although he was
backed by Cardinal Beaufort, he was strongly
opposed by Humphrey, Duke of Gloucester,
last surviving brother of Henry V, who
considered that any peaceful move towards
England's old enemy amounted to treachery.

Suffolk was forty-eight years of age at this
time but showed no signs of diminishing
strength in body or mind. He was well-built,
bearded and fresh-complexioned and while
he disciplined his household with a control
that irked many of his younger knights he
subjected himself to a no less vigorous
routine. He had married Alice Chaucer,

granddaughter of the poet, in 1430 and they had one son, John. William's last act before sailing to France had been to set in motion the betrothal of this child to the daughter of his friend John, Duke of Somerset. John had been tragically killed while out hunting and William had been appointed guardian of the three-year-old Margaret Beaufort. There could be no surer sign of William's faith in the future when he attempted to ally himself by marriage to the most powerful family in England.

In the castle of Montil-les-Tours he, with Charles VII and the Duke of Orleans, now awaited the arrival of René, Isabella and their daughter.

'The child is a niece of my wife,' the King of France was telling his companions, 'but I have not seen her for some time and so cannot therefore vouch for her looks or her intelligence.'

Suffolk, noting that this remark was typical of the man whom Joan of Arc had succeeded in establishing upon the throne of France, made some polite rejoinder that he was quite sure that Margaret of Anjou would live up to the constant rumours he had heard of her talents and good looks.

Orleans, his long, expressive face registering the gallantry which twenty years of imprisonment in England had failed to stamp out, stated that he had heard Margaret was charming and artistic and a fit match for the scholarly Henry.

'But my dear fellow,' the French king said with a knowing wink for Suffolk, 'you would think a peasant girl from wildest Brittany attractive after your enforced detention in England among the — '

'The English nobility, which is noted for its patrician features?' Orleans supplied mildly and without undue haste. It would not do to offend the proud Suffolk at this moment when their hopes were centred on bringing an end to the bitter warfare which had existed for over a hundred years between their two countries. Horse-faced some of the English might be but they had their attractions and Orleans had not found them wanting in their attempts to alleviate his sufferings. There had been that little Jane Beaufort who had married James I of Scotland; she had been a beauty, with no mistake, and many an hour had he and James spent in their small, turreted room in Windsor making verses to her charms. To change the subject he turned to speak to Pierre de Brézé, formerly Steward of Poitou and now Chamberlain to the French King, a man of medium stature, dark of hair and complexion with the bearing of a military man. Pierre de Brézé broke off his conversation with Dr. Adam Moleyns to answer Orleans just as a herald announced the arrival of the Duke of Anjou and his wife and daughter; so it was that the first person Margaret saw as she entered the presence chamber was Pierre and as she answered his welcoming smile with a tight movement of her lips some measure of strength flowed into her. By such small actions of fate are our destinies sealed.

René led his daughter with her hand on his arm to curtsy to Charles who came down from the velvet-covered chair set high on a dais to welcome his guests. The King kissed René on both cheeks and took Margaret's hand in his own. 'May I present the Earl of Suffolk, emissary of our beloved cousin of England,' he said and drew Suffolk towards the dais. The warmth of his voice portrayed his pleasure in his niece and Orleans noted with satisfaction that Margaret was very much more comely and attractive than he had dared hope; his spies had not coloured the picture for him.

Suffolk, in his turn, as he paid his respects to the future Queen of England, was delighted with the girl who graciously received his words of address and answered them without a trace of nervousness. If Henry was not moved from his celibacy by this dainty morsel of femininity he should have been the monk that his enemies stated — too frequently for comfort — was his true occupation. Margaret gave, on first acquaintance, an appearance of lusty, wholesome womanhood which was exactly what the realm of England needed to provide a string of sturdy heirs who would ensure the continuity of the Lancastrian succession for generations to come. As the conversation became general and Isabella was drawn into the circle Charles moved about his court making introductions: Suffolk and Orleans smiled at one another; their task was easier than they had imagined.

Events moved swiftly during the following two days and René, buoyed by the obvious approval with which Margaret had been received by Henry's ambassador, was as eager as the other participants to conclude the truce. On the twenty second day of May the final decisions were made and it was arranged that a betrothal service should take place in the church of St. Martin two days later.

To Margaret time seemed to melt into a continuous round of excitement in which she was the nub, the centre about which all else revolved. It was at one and the same moment exhilerating and a little frightening but it gave her no leisure to think of anything but which gown she should choose for the ceremony and make endless conversation with the nobility of England who had come on their king's behalf. Margaret discovered that Suffolk was a man of kind disposition who studied her every want while Dr. Moleyns, Sir Robert Roos, Dr. Richard Andrews, who was secretary to King Henry, and other members of the English court were learned and courteous men far removed from the boorish ignoramuses she had expected. If Henry proved as interesting and was loving and warm into the bargain her future looked bright indeed.

The day of the betrothal was warm with brilliant sunshine which sparkled on the jewels of the courtiers as they crowded into the church to witness the union between the English king and the Angevin princess. The ceremony was performed by Peter de Monte, Bishop of Brescia, who waited at the porch with William de la Pole and the King of France for Margaret and her father.

When the formal words of betrothal had been spoken between Suffolk, as Henry's proxy, and Margaret they were led down the aisle to the sound of a fanfare of trumpets. At the altar rail they partook of communion together and then shared in the elaborate service of chanting and prayers which followed.

It was evening before the wedding party came to the abbey of St. Justin where an enormous banquet, at René's expense, had been prepared. While mountains of food were demolished a troupe of itinerant players acted some light-hearted scenes in which camels picked their heavy-footed way across the sanded floor of the great hall and giants disguised as trees tried to impede the progress of the knights on their extraordinary steeds. Margaret joined in the laughter of the rest of the noble company but wished that they might not protract the playlets for too long for dancing was to follow the banquet and she preferred this type of entertainment above all others.

René, who had been, in truth, hard pressed to find sufficient money to pay for this elaborate celebration had nevertheless stinted nothing and the musicians he had hired were the best Tours could boast. Margaret danced several measures before a strange voice requested her company for a pavanne.

'Monsieur de Brézé?' she asked in a questioning tone as the soldier statesman stood before her.

'At your service, madame, now and always,' Pierre said with a bow and before she could refuse had taken her hand and led her out to join the others. His grasp was strong, reassuring and his palms dry; a fact which pleased Margaret for she was more used to the sweaty hands of the pages at Angers. Where, she found herself asking, was Louis? She had completely forgotten him in the excitement of the past days. In the next half an hour she was to be given cause to think of him less.

Pierre de Brézé was an accomplished dancer, moving with a grace not usually associated with a man who lived his life in the saddle and who had fought the English from his native soil since he had been old enough to wield a lance. Not as smooth-tongued as Orleans, who had almost overwhelmed her with compliments and classical references to the goddesses of Greece, he was well spoken and an interesting talker. Not until he had partnered Margaret for ten minutes or so did he mention her forthcoming journey to England.

'You are looking forward to being Queen of England?'

'Do not all young girls dream of being a queen?' she parried.

'Probably; but not all of them are called upon to fulfil that high destiny. I take it that you are not afraid of the prospect; I am right,

26

am I not?' Margaret nodded. 'Well, tell me what you know of Henry.'

'He is young, kind and a man of great devotion to God.'

'And you think this will make him a good husband?' In anyone else Margaret would have found this conversation impertinent but she liked this clean-featured man and enjoyed the close proximity of his body; he was at one and the same time both disturbing and reassuring.

'I hope so,' she said simply.

Pierre regarded her frankly, restraining himself with difficulty from tilting her chin to look into her marvellous eyes and kiss her parted lips. 'If you should ever find otherwise,' he said hoarsely, 'I'm your man in life and limb.'

'Do you think I am in any peril?' she asked quickly.

'Oh, no,' he responded with more ease, 'with my lord of Suffolk and Cardinal Beaufort as strong allies of the King and yourself you have nothing to fear.'

'But my marriage is to honour the truce between the French and the English, is it not? You do not try to warn me that I have other causes to thank?'

For a brief moment Pierre considered the prospect of lying to the girl so trustingly enjoying his company and found he could not bring himself to betray her. 'Henry has enemies and no heir. If you have not heard already that he has ministers who consider peace with France an anathema you will soon learn about them when you move among court circles in England. The most powerful advocate of continuing the war is your Henry's paternal uncle, Humphrey, Duke of Gloucester.'

'I suppose that is natural,' Margaret said, 'when one considers that he is a brother of Henry V.'

'Of course,' Pierre agreed. The music stopped and he hastily asked Margaret if she would care for some wine from the void table which had been set up against the kitchen screens at the far end of the hall from the dais. She accepted with alacrity for she was deeply anxious to hear more of what she realized was an unbiased account of her future in England.

Pierre found two hannaps of wine and he and Margaret sat down together in a deep embrasure. 'Is there any other reason why Duke Humphrey is opposed to the peace plan — and my marriage?'

Pierre was frank. 'Yes, there is; you will not remember, of course, and I must confess that my knowledge is only what I have heard from my parents and the French court, but Edward III (of foul memory, here in France!) had four sons. Of these John of Gaunt was not the eldest but was certainly the most powerful after Edward the Black Prince died in 1376. This John of Gaunt had two — or perhaps it was three — families; of the first his son became Henry IV and of the second another son became the Cardinal Beaufort of whom you have heard so much.'

'So Duke Humphrey and Cardinal Beaufort are descended from the same family but there is a rivalry between them?'

'Yes, that is absolutely so,' Pierre said with what he recognized was relief. If his companion was as quick-witted as she appeared she could face the future without fear. He took the shapely hand which lay in her lap and held it to his mouth. 'You learn fast, little queen, and I am glad.'

'I am used to factions, as you must well know, for my father has been at odds with my lord Burgundy for years and he tells me you have supported our own king in his troubles with the Dauphin and his adherents. Do not forget that I spent quite a part of my childhood besieged in Naples; my mother was a fearless soldier, I can tell you.'

'She is a redoubtable woman, is our Isabella, and she is blessed with the most beautiful daughter in Christendom.'

'Now you sound like Orleans,' Margaret said with a little grimace.

'And you do not care for compliments?'

'Not when they are as smooth as his.'

'But mine are those of a rough soldier who means what he says.'

'Are you married?'

'Aye.'

'Where is your wife?' Margaret bent forward, surveying the vast concourse of people.

'Not here; she is at home caring for our children.'

'I see. Perhaps you would be kind enough to escort me back to the high table; it would not do for me to be seen to spend too much time in your company.'

Pierre arose at once, greeting a pleasant, plump woman who passed as he turned to take Margaret's hand.

'Who is that?' she asked.

'That's Agnes Sorel, the mistress of Charles.'

'But she looks so nice,' Margaret burst out before she could stop herself. Pierre chuckled. 'My sweet innocent, she is not only pleasant but the best influence on the king that France could possibly have. Many of us here owe much to that kindly soul.'

Margaret was immediately and irrationally jealous and attempted to show her displeasure by snatching her hand away. Pierre, as if he divined her thoughts, only held her the tighter. As he made his polite farewells he whispered, 'She may well be the best influence but I still contend that you are the loveliest queen in Europe and I would that I were king of England.'

Margaret returned to the dais slightly bemused and had some difficulty in replying to René's enquiries about her prolonged absence. This was a fine time to find a married man attractive. She spent the rest of the evening with her eyes demurely downcast and was attentive and courteous to the emissaries of her future husband. It would never do for Henry to hear rumours that she was flippant or unchaste.

She did not know whether to be glad or sorry on the following morning when Isabella came to tell her that they were returning immediately to Angers for an indefinite time. On balance it might have been easier to have journeyed straight to England. But diplomatic bargaining did not allow for personal feelings and she had yet to discover that France intended to levy more from Henry and his ministers than the truce which her betrothal had sealed.

It was not until the following December that Suffolk, who had gone to England to report the success of his mission in the matter of the King's marriage, was able to return to France with an immense entourage for the purpose of escorting Margaret to her husband.

Margaret, and many Englishmen, could not discover if the delay in her departure was a scheme cannily hatched by her father and his overlord, the King of France, to extract further concessions from Henry or whether it was that the two Frenchmen were so engaged in the reduction of the city of Metz that they had no time available for anything else.

Whatever the reason Margaret was not allowed to see the English Ambassador and was kept in one of her mother's castles in Lorraine while the splendid train of nobles were entertained (at Charles of France's expense) in Nancy. To say that Margaret was puzzled was certainly true for she could not reconcile her peace-loving father with the attack upon Metz and she had heard rumours that Henry was being asked to cede Le Mans and other territories held by the English in France as part of the marriage settlement.

As far as her personal feelings were involved Margaret had ceased to mind one way or the other by the end of March for she was now torn in two by her wish to please her parents by going to England and by her desire to remain in France with them. That this last wish had anything to do with Pierre de Brézé she would have been reluctant to admit but was aware that when he came to René's court her heart beat faster and the day was that much more pleasant. Adult enough to realize that this was the first time her emotions had been aroused she was young enough to imagine situations when he became her champion and carried her off from the clutches of dragons and such on a white steed. Of Henry of England she thought hardly at all.

Eventually René and Charles of France succeeded in subduing Metz and could turn to the business of the proxy marriage of René's daughter.

Never had a more glittering company of nobles come together in Nancy and such was the scope of the truce which had been negotiated that Philip of Burgundy was among the guests. To honour Suffolk, now a marquis, and his English companions eight days of feasting and jousting were offered and once Margaret and Suffolk had been united in the cathedral of Nancy by the Bishop of Toul the splendid series of entertainments commenced.

The women of the various courts grasped the opportunity of showing off their most gorgeous finery but Isabella wisely told her daughter to wear only the simplest of gowns and rely upon her young beauty to outshine them all. That this advice had something to do with the depleted state of René's coffers there could be no doubt but it was also true that Margaret needed no embellishment to enhance her lush beauty. With a crown of real marguerites entwined in her flowing hair she was a match for any painted female from Paris or London.

Suffolk had brought his wife with him to bring back their new queen and Margaret was drawn to the stately woman who, while paying her respects, smiled and told her that she hoped Margaret would look upon her as a second mother when the time came to part with Isabella. Feast followed feast and tournament crowded upon joust as the days passed until on the afternoon before Margaret was to leave on her journey to England Pierre de Brézé challenged the archers of Suffolk's escort to a trial of skill with the archers of France. This, a competition which had had more deadly purposes in the not too distant past, was hailed as a sign of security in the truce and the lists were immediately filled. Pierre himself gave the thousand crowns which formed the prize.

The day of the contest was full of the promise of summer and the company took their places in the tilt yard of the castle to encourage their representatives. Court jesters took upon themselves the business of placing the odds and announced as the first two men took up their places that the English were clear favourites.

Margaret sat with her mother and father, Suffolk and Charles of France while at the other end of the royal box were Burgundy, Foix, René's brother and a host of ladies among whom was Agnes Sorel. This lady had delighted the company two days earlier when she had dressed as a knight in a suit of armour covered in jewels and had challenged any man present to unhorse her from her white charger. Margaret had been aware that the matrons of the company had looked upon this daring behaviour as shocking but the men had regarded the king's mistress with open admiration. Unable to help herself Margaret craned forward now to see if Pierre were among the admirers clustered about Agnes and was relieved to discover he was not.

When the horn sounded for the championship to begin Margaret saw that Pierre was close behind the trumpeter seated on a roan stallion she had not seen before. She prepared to enjoy the contest and soon caught the enthusiasm of the crowds. It was during the fifth or sixth bout that she found Pierre standing at her elbow.

'Give me one of the daisies from your bouquet and there will be no doubt of the outcome,' he whispered.

Obediently she tugged a pink-tipped flower from the posy in her lap and silently handed it to him; as their fingers met he slipped something into her hand. 'Wear this,' he said softly, 'and should you ever have need of me send it to me with a trusted messenger and I shall be at your side as swiftly as ship and horse will bring me.'

Before she had time to speak he had gone and was once more at his place in the lists. When a great cheer marked a French archer she opened her fist and looked down on a ring set with a blue stone in which a tiny circle of pearls formed a daisy. With a catch of her breath she put it on the smallest finger of her right hand and felt tears sting her eyes.

Contrary to what was expected the French won the competition and in the merriment which followed Margaret made her excuses to her father and, calling the lady in waiting who had been assigned to her, went to her rooms.

She must make special preparation to look her best for this, her last night at the French court; but if she hoped that she would be able to flirt a little with Pierre she was disappointed for he was nowhere to be seen in the crowded hall. Margaret sat next to the Dauphine at the feast. 'So you go to England while I remain here,' this Scottish girl said during the course of the long meal.

'Do you envy me?' Margaret asked.

'I do not know how to answer you,' the Dauphine replied with a sigh, 'for as I watch you and your family I am certain you are as devoted to your family as I was to mine and it comes very hard to leave a doting father.'

'Your father was James I?'

'Yes, the great friend of Orleans.'

'Was your mother not a Beaufort?'

'Indeed yes and did much to patch a truce between England and Scotland.'

'It did not last?' Margaret asked swiftly. The Dauphine was overcome with a bout of coughing which left her breathless but she at length said drily: 'Hereditary enemies are slow to make lasting peace; be very wary, cousin, in the ponderous matter of statesmanship. I thank God and Holy Mary that I have not much longer to try and keep a balance between Louis and his father.'

'Don't say that!' Margaret cried.

'I am quite resigned to dying and since my father was so cruelly murdered I have no wish to return to Scotland. But come, this is foolish talk to a bride and I hope you will forgive me; I spoke only to tell you that you are not the first girl to be snatched from her family in the interests of her country's future. I pray that you may be more successful than I.'

'Am I right in believing that there were Scottish archers among those competing in the Sire de Brézé's contest this afternoon?' Margaret said to lighten the tone of this unexpected conversation.

'Indeed they were and I should like to think they helped to win; they are doughty fighters, the Scots, and hate your country of adoption as much as do the French. Why is it, do you think, that men cannot live together without fighting?'

'God only knows, but at least you and I are playing our part in helping them to learn.'

38

3

The leavetaking between Margaret, her sister and her mother was painful but Margaret did her best to maintain some kind of composure before she joined the brilliant company that was to escort her on her long journey into England. When she mounted the saddle of the best horse René had been able to muster from his stables she saw that most of the nobility who had attended her nuptials were to go with her as she headed north; it was an honour indeed to have the King of France among this number. She could not be other than flattered and delighted.

René came with her as far as Bar-le-Duc and here she was unable to fight back the tears and clung to him as if she were going to lifelong imprisonment; only the presence of her brother John of Calabria saved her from breaking down completely. It was useless for René to tell her he would send heralds with frequent messages for she could see and hear nothing but her grief. Not for the first time she wished that Pierre de Brézé sat among the nobles who watched her cry upon her father's shoulders; if he were with her as she went on to Paris she would have made a better attempt to be brave.

From Paris, where her brother turned for home, Orleans rode with Suffolk and the cream of the English court until they came to the borders of the English possessions where Richard, Duke of York, Governor of Normandy received her. Margaret felt as if she were on alien territory already but it was a welcome change from the monotonous jogging in the saddle. Margaret sank into the feather mattress in her small cabin and was instantly asleep.

The women of her entourage were aroused in the chilly watches before dawn by her cries of distress and hurriedly dragged blankets about them as they rushed to her aid. They found her clutching her stomach and crying out as waves of nausea and pain made her almost lose consciousness. Lady Suffolk and the Countess of Salisbury exchanged glances of dismay for this was not a happy welcome to English territory and boded ill for the state entrance into Rouen on the following afternoon. One of Margaret's ladies sent a page for her personal physician while Lady Isabel Grey quietly found a silver basin and unhurriedly proffered it to her at the exact moment she was violently sick. Margaret looked at the comely woman with her long fair hair in disarray down her back and tried to express her gratitude before another bout of pain made her moan and sweat.

It was some hours before Margaret was at ease and Lady Suffolk and Isabel Grey volunteered to sit with the suffering girl while Rose Merston, a maid of the bedchamber, found them blankets and hot mugs of milk and wine to sustain them against the chill of an early spring night.

Margaret was not well enough to appear for the state entrance into the capital of Normandy and Suffolk decided that the Countess of Salisbury should take her place.

'You are about the same height and build and dressed in the queen's robes I defy anyone to know the difference,' he said with a chuckle. 'I'm glad now that Richard of York arranged that this pageant should be on the river.'

The entire party were destined to stay aboard the barge for some seven days and nights while Suffolk and the rest of the English entourage awaited Margaret's return to health and the arrival of money from England to pay for the Queen's passage across the Channel. Suffolk kept this last detail from his royal charge and made out that as the queen was indisposed only the finest ship would suit his rigorous requirements for her conveyance. Eventually heralds came from the King of England with sufficient funds to pay those who had waited upon the escort in France and the master of the cog '*John of Cherbourg*'. This sturdy little vessel was lying at Harfleur and it was here that Margaret and her suite embarked.

Despite having recovered sufficiently to visit goldsmiths in Rouen and display concern for the poor of that city by distributing alms Margaret was brought low again as soon as the ship put out of the harbour and was so ill with the motion of the ship in the rough seas that she wished several times that she might die as had the little Dauphine soon after they had parted in Nancy. What a pity that sturdy sons of the family could not be spared to make diplomatic marriages.

At last on the morning of April 9th the battered cog put into Porchester. Margaret was so weak that she was unable to stand without assistance. When Lady Suffolk told her husband this distressing fact he came himself to her cabin and lifted her from her bunk as if she were a fledgling bird and carried her down the gangplank to the shore. From the outset their destinies in England were interwoven. Heralds who had come to welcome the ship informed Suffolk and his train of nobles that Henry awaited his bride in Porchester castle and he now stowed Margaret in a closed litter and saw to the disposition of her ladies and household on the horses and chariots put at their disposal. While he was so engaged a gust of wind blew his hat from his head and sent veils flying and pennants streaming; almost at once there was a clap of thunder and rain fell from dense black clouds which scudded low in the threatening sky. The superstitious read omens and others crossed themselves hurriedly; England in April it might be but an unpropitious moment for the heavens to declare themselves in conflict.

Yet, when Margaret had been bathed and attired in fresh clothing, the sun shone from a cloudless blue sky and all the song birds of Hampshire seemed united in chorus at Porchester castle. She remarked upon the freshness of the new leaves upon the trees and the clusters of primroses in the banked lawn under her window. 'Just like home,' she said, 'and were the streets really lined with cheering people or did I imagine it?'

'You did not imagine it, your grace,' Rose Merston told her, 'and they threw flowers in your path all the way; 'twas a pity you were not well enough to see it.'

'I am better now,' Margaret told her crisply.

'I have had enough of illness these past weeks to last me a lifetime. If it were not sufficient to suffer *mal de mer* on that atrocious sea it was the last straw to have Master Fransico, my physician, think I was sickening for the smallpox. Is there a mirror unpacked that I may see if my cheeks are as pale as they feel?'

She was pale it was true but the hideous spots which had broken out almost as soon as she had boarded the cog had disappeared leaving her skin unblemished. Margaret sighed with relief and stood still while her women dressed her in her most becoming gown and braided her newly washed hair. As she did so she rehearsed some of the thousands of things which René and King Charles had impressed upon her during the ride from Nancy northwards through France. One or two of these strange instructions had worried her during her illness and she had had nightmares concerning the new responsibilities thrust upon her but now on this lovely spring morning she felt able to face the strange young man with whom she would soon be sharing the most intimate of human relationships and would learn to see England through his eyes. Her women had almost completed her toilette when Rose came to say that my lord of Suffolk was at the door with a squire of the King's who wished to give the queen a letter.

'Bid him enter,' Margaret said and took a last look in her silver mirror; she had hardly time to take in the strangeness of her piled hair when Suffolk came in and took her hand to kiss. The squire, a gangling young man, fell on his knees, giving her a folded missive and a leather-covered box. Margaret read the letter, written in a scholarly script, and smiled at the wishes from Henry that she might be as happy to be in their realm as he was to welcome her. 'Shall I open the box?' she asked Suffolk.

'Of course, your grace, it is my lord's wedding gift to you.'

Margaret could not stop the little cry of delight which rose to her throat as she saw the magnificent ring set with a great, glowing ruby. 'How wonderful; I have never possessed such a jewel before.'

'The King's grace wished you to have it for it was given to him by his uncle the Cardinal when he was a lad of some twelve summers.' Suffolk did not think it was the moment to mention that the great ruby had been a gift from Henry Beaufort to his grand-nephew on the occasion of his coronation in Paris when he took to himself the title of King of France. The queen would learn soon enough the complexities of her high rank and this day was to be one of pleasure.

'Will you convey to my lord my sincere gratitude and tell him that I hope to thank him personally in a short time.' Suffolk bowed and he and the squire withdrew. The door had hardly closed upon them when Suffolk returned and came to the queen.

'My lady,' he said, with a chuckle, 'what did you think of the squire who brought you the letter?'

'The squire, my lord? Why, I did not notice him as I was too intent upon reading the message and studying the jewel which my husband has sent.'

'That squire, your grace, *was* your husband,' Suffolk said.

'Oh, how could I have let him stay thus upon his knees without so much as a glance!' Margaret blushed with shame at her gaffe but Suffolk took her hand and patted it in a paternal manner. 'My lady, it was the king's wish to visit you and I can promise you he was delighted with your acceptance of his gift.'

Alice, Suffolk's wife, came into the room to announce that the king was ready to receive his bride and, when told of the joke Henry had played upon Margaret, said in an aside to Lady Isabel Grey she trusted that it might be the beginning of a change in the sober young man and that the coming of the queen would mean less of the austere life for Henry.

As Suffolk put Margaret's hand upon his arm and her suite formed up in procession behind them Lady Grey said in an undertone that she hoped this might be so indeed. 'Do you remember that disastrous Yuletide when Buckingham tried to liven the proceedings somewhat and brought in that troupe of gipsies? I shall never forget the king's face when he saw the bared bosoms of the women dancers.'

'I was not present,' Alice said, 'but I cannot believe his grace remained to watch the performance.'

'No, he did not. I think he was hardly twenty at the time but he turned away and stalked out of the hall. It threw the court into some confusion,' Lady Grey chuckled, 'for no one knew whether to stay or follow the king.'

★   ★   ★

As she walked beside the sturdy and dependable Suffolk Margaret was trying desperately to remember the young squire who had so gallantly knelt to her but could recall nothing except that he was dressed in crimson velvet and had fairish rather lank hair. If only she had thought to look well upon the man she would be spared much of the coming ordeal; yet it was pleasing to know that even if he were a king he was human enough to play japes and be anxious to see what Suffolk had brought him home.

When she came into the audience chamber there seemed to be a great crush of people, some like Moleyns, Lord Clifford, Sir Richard Roos and Sir Thomas Stanley whom she mercifully recognized as companions from her journey to England; but there were others, total strangers, who regarded her more intently. There appeared to be no sign of the crimson-suited squire who had knelt to her hardly half-an-hour before. Had he spent the intervening time, as she had, dressing himself in his most gorgeous raiment to greet her? When a tall, pale-faced young man dressed in the simple garb of a country squire came up to her and spoke her name she nodded to him, distantly, and prepared to follow Suffolk further into the crowded room. To her astonishment Suffolk did not move but brought her face to face with the gangling young man.

'My liege, this is the queen.' He stepped back, his pride in his protégé apparent in his voice.

'My lady Margaret, you are most welcome,

both to this court and to this realm. May God bless your coming and keep you here in peace.'

Margaret bowed her head and made a deep curtsy, noting, even in this momentous moment, that Henry wore boots so stout that they would have suited a farmer trudging through the midden. This was not — this could not be the king! While she fought the mingled shock and overwhelming disappointment that threatened to bring on a recurrence of her sickness Margaret found herself lifted by a hand soft as a woman's. 'Do not kneel, my lady, you are my queen; come, and I shall introduce you to my uncle.' Henry led her towards the far end of the room where a number of prelates and other dignitaries stood watching the king make the acquaintance of his new wife. As Henry and Margaret approached, one man clad in the scarlet of a cardinal detached himself and came towards them holding out both hands.

'My lady, may I present my esteemed grand-uncle, Henry, Bishop of Winchester and a cardinal of Rome; uncle, this is my beloved consort, Margaret, daughter of the noble René of Anjou and Isabella of Lorraine. Pray that she may receive as much comfort from you as I have done in the past.'

While Beaufort smiled at her with great

warmth and spoke to her unaffectedly Margaret studied this elder statesman who had been largely concerned in the matter of securing her hand for Henry and found that although he was approaching his seventieth year he held himself proudly making it impossible not to recognize the once noble frame. His eyes were brilliant in their sunken sockets and were so compelling that, with the fine carving of his hooked nose, they drew attention from his flabby jowls. Although he had an air of great importance which was manifested in the rich silk of his clothes and the flashing jewels upon his fingers he spoke to Margaret in the most gentle voice and made it apparent to her that in his choice of bride for his nephew he had been proved right. He continued at her side as Henry moved on to present Margaret to Bishops Ayscough and Kemp, a number of other nobles whom she vainly tried to impress upon her memory and the wives of some of the men who had brought her to England.

Used as she was to the turmoil of court life Margaret found she was soon exhausted with greeting so many new faces; she put it down to the fact that she was still weak from her illness and the strain of speaking the language which was not yet as fluent as her lessons with her tutor had promised. Yet she knew that underlying these obvious reasons for her fatigue was the shock she had received when she had realised that she was tied for life to a man who, at first sight, seemed but a soft youth who roused in her no physical attraction whatsoever. She, who had so hoped to be married to a man lusty in sport and in bed, had been sold to a weakling who would have been more at home in a monastery than a court. Whether she would or not, a picture of Pierre de Brézé in the lists at Nancy sprang into her mind and she saw again his powerful shoulders, lithe body and quick, intelligent eyes. She pushed away the remembrance and concentrated on making the favourable impression which, her father had instilled in her, was absolutely essential; she must not fail in the first hour of her presentation to the court of England.

★ ★ ★

Margaret and Henry were formally married by Bishop Ayscough of Salisbury in Tichfield Abbey; a ceremony marked by no special display but one that she would never forget even if only for the sight of Henry's face as she had joined him at the porch door. As she had approached on Suffolk's arm the king had stared at her and she had seen a sudden

51

widening of his eyes before he had hastily looked down at the ground and closed his hand about hers.

Yet it did not seem as they wound their slow way to London that Henry was in haste to consummate their marriage for she slept alone, always in the best chamber that the castle or hospice could muster, but nevertheless by herself. More than once she cried herself to sleep and several times was bitterly disappointed when Henry paid her much attention during the day but failed to come near her when once they had made their formal goodnights at the supper table. She was honest enough to realise that it was not desire which prompted her to want Henry near her but loneliness.

At Shene, where they spent the last night before entering London, Margaret plaintively asked Alice de la Pole, as she attended her solitary retirement, where Henry might be at this hour.

Alice looked at her and then hastily busied herself with laying jewellery in a velvet-covered box. 'No doubt his grace is at his prayers, my lady; I saw him bound for the chapel with his confessor as I came to your room.' Alice shut the box with a decisive snap and then came round to stand beside Margaret who sat disconsolate on the side of her canopied bed. 'Will you forgive me if I say something which is in my mind?'

'But of course! You know me well enough, surely to realise that I am only too anxious to hear your advice and reflections. Tell me what you wish.'

'Well,' Alice began slowly, 'I hope very much that your grace will not prejudge the king too hastily in the matter of his apparent tortoise-like approach to the royal bed but I would have you understand that he has not had the usual upbringing of a prince of the royal blood. I know you are very well aware of his precipitation to the throne when he was but nine months of age but I think it is worth considering for a moment or two what that really meant in human terms. You, despite your father's imprisonment at the hands of Burgundy, have nevertheless enjoyed a wholesome childhood with a loving pair of parents who ensured that you enjoyed family life as well as learnt to fit yourself for the great role which you are now called upon to play. With his grace it was never thus.'

'But he did not lose his mother,' Margaret cried.

'He did, if not by death, by the cruel actions of Humphrey of Gloucester.'

'How could that be?'

'When Henry V died he left a will stating

53

that his two brothers Bedford and Gloucester should be regents of England and his territories in France during your husband's minority but Gloucester was only to serve when Bedford was detained in France to wage war. Gloucester was always jealous of his elder brother and lost no opportunity when Bedford was called abroad to wield his authority. In the matter of Henry's widow he seemed more stubborn and unkind than necessary, especially when his own marriages had left a great deal to be desired — ,'

'What did he do?'

'From the outset after Henry V's death he appointed tutors for the upbringing of the infant king and gradually deprived Katherine de Valois of the company of her baby so that she became a lonely, deserted young woman. Perhaps not surprisingly, she did not remain thus for long and she fell in love with the Master of her Wardrobe, a young squire of her late husband named Owen Tudor. When she was exiled to Hatfield Owen went with her and she bore him five children.'

'Bastards?' Margaret asked.

'I believe not, for it was generally understood that the couple married secretly. Whatever the facts Humphrey lost no time in separating the lovers and Queen Katherine died in Bermondsey Abbey not long afterwards.'

'Did my husband not know of this?'

'No, but it was the discovery of Humphrey's cruelty which set him against him forever; I do not believe he has ever forgiven him for his mother's death.'

'Poor Henry, I am so glad that you have told me of this for it helps me to understand him a little the more. I feel almost guilty that I have enjoyed such a happy childhood when he was so deprived.'

'Do not think he suffered as far as schooling and such were concerned,' Alice put in with haste, 'for Lord Warwick saw to it that he had the best tutors; I should say that what he lacked was the mothering and the womanly touch. You do understand what I am trying to tell you, don't you?'

'Of course,' Margaret said, 'and shall sleep the better for the knowledge. One thing I must ask, however; are Henry's half-brothers at Court? I do not remember being presented to them.'

'His grace has done everything to remedy his uncle's misdemeanours and has personally provided for the young Tudors; you will doubtless meet Edmund and Jasper at your Coronation for they are more often than not at court these days.'

'I am so glad that you have spoken out to me on this matter,' Margaret said and climbed into her lonely bed. 'I am most fortunate to have friends like you and Lord William.'

'Long may we serve your graces. Goodnight my lady.'

4

On the wide expanse of Blackheath Margaret and Henry were met by the Duke of Gloucester and five hundred of his retainers dressed in new livery in honour of the occasion.

Humphrey rode towards them and dismounted to bow humbly to his nephew and his bride. Margaret, eager to evaluate this man who had been so much against her marriage, studied him as he spoke pleasantly enough to Henry and herself. She saw that this last surviving brother of Henry V had been an undoubtedly handsome man but his face bore unmistakable signs of the dissolute life which Suffolk and his wife had been at pains to recount. Humphrey had beautiful hands which he used to emphasise his smooth and fluent speech. His eyes were heavily-lidded, a cool grey that was almost colourless, and his mouth thin. His dress was rich, in the latest fashion and sewn in many places with precious stones. He gave every appearance of conforming to the description Suffolk had given her of a man who had been bursting with energy in his youth and through the thwarting of his ambitions to rule England had become vain, selfish and greedy. Had Suffolk told the truth? It was difficult for a girl of fifteen with little experience to judge but Margaret knew that Suffolk's portrayal of her husband as a glowing, vital youth had been sadly astray and it was possible that he had erred in his description of the Duke of Gloucester.

At Placentia, Humphrey's palace at Greenwich, there seemed no evidence of Suffolk's claims and Henry and Margaret were shown every courtesy and patience. When Margaret was told of Humphrey's library and expressed a wish to visit it she was taken to see this prize possession of Gloucester's with obvious pleasure. As she listened to the ageing Duke in his enthusiasm for the magnificent illuminations which he showed her it was difficult to reconcile this scholar with the cruel despot who had parted Katherine de Valois and her second husband. Yet René had specifically warned her to be on guard for ingratiating behaviour in any of her subjects. Could it be that Gloucester was trying just a little too hard to please? Was not the lavish hospitality and the wearing of a marguerite by every member of his household somewhat overstating his penitence? Time alone would tell and now she could do no more than enjoy the entertainment which was offered.

Greenwich, set on a bank sloping down to the river Thames, was almost as pleasant as any chateau on the Loire and Humphrey had spared no expense in the laying out of the gardens: Margaret walked with her ladies in lilac-scented courtyards and listened to the music of Humphrey's musicians. If this was typical of England she had not much to fear; even Henry's reluctance to share her bed lost its frustration and she basked in the compliments showered upon her.

It was during the two days they spent at Greenwich that Alice Suffolk brought her own dressmaker to Margaret and told her that it was the king's wish that his bride should have several new gowns for her coronation fetes. In truth Henry had willingly enough agreed that he should delve into his already depleted coffers to give Margaret a more suitable wardrobe than René had been able to supply but the idea had come from the Suffolks rather than the king himself. It was difficult to persuade a man who dressed simply himself that his wife's gowns would be the laughing stock of the English ladies of the court who so keenly waited to greet Margaret on her arrival in London. Margaret entered into the scheme with the greatest of pleasure and chose tawny silks and golden and cream brocades to complement her dark auburn hair and it was in a dress of palest yellow that she rode into Southwark to shouts of welcome from the citizens. Through streets lined with people and bright with wreaths of hedgerow flowers she and Henry, smiling with pleasure, made their way to London bridge where pageants and tableaux were enacted and flimsily dressed maidens addressed them with lyrical verses. All the houses on the narrow bridge were hung with tapestries or brightly coloured banners and from the windows men and women waved and shouted good wishes.

Before they were formally welcomed by the mayor and the masters of the livery companies, resplendent in their blue gowns and red hoods with sleeves embroidered to show their trade, Margaret heard a golden-haired girl expound her virtues in a poem especially written by Lydgate for the great day of her coming to the heart of England.

'Most Christian princess, by influence of grace,
 Daughter of Jerusalem, our pleasure
And joy, welcome as ever Princess was,
With hearts entire and whole affiance;
Causer of wealth, joy and abundance
Your city, your people, your subjects all,

With heart, with word, with deed, your
    highness to advance,
Welcome, Welcome! Welcome unto you
    all.'

'And may I echo those sentiments,' Henry
said taking her hand and putting it to his lips.
'I pray that your entrance to this our city of
London may be the beginning of peace and
prosperity to our realm. I thank you, with all
my heart, for doing me the honour of
becoming my queen.'

'Thank you,' Margaret said and pressed the
fingers encircling her own. She was rewarded
with a swift smile and a look of unfeigned
gratitude. The day seemed suddenly more
fair.

The progress throughout the day was
marked by recitals at Cornhill, Cheapside and
at Paul's gate where they were to lodge for the
night but Margaret was not tired; she felt
exhilarated by the obvious approbation of the
Londoners and the happy omen which had
marked the exchange of intimate glances
between herself and Henry. Nor was she to be
disappointed for later Henry asked if he
might visit her in her chamber.

Margaret prepared herself for bed with
extra care, having her maids brush her hair
until it shone and scenting her skin with the

precious vial of essences that had been her mother's last gift before they parted. She awaited Henry in a mixture of pleasurable excitement and dread, sternly closing her mind to what might have been her feelings had it been Pierre who came to claim her for his own.

When almost an hour and a half had gone by since she had climbed into her ornately draped bed Margaret began to feel drowsy, wondering if perhaps she had misinterpreted the meaning of Henry's murmured words. She was about to turn on her side with a reluctant belief that this was indeed the case when the door of her bedchamber was opened abruptly, closed softly and feet shuffled across the polished wood floor.

'My dear?' Henry asked, almost in hesitation.

'Henry?' she said, fighting the stupor of half-sleep.

'May I come in with you?'

'Of course.'

Margaret heard the thud of his heavy bedgown as it fell to the floor and felt the feather mattress sink as it took Henry's weight. She held her breath as he moved gingerly towards her and put out a cold and thin arm to encircle her waist; without realising she did so she held her breath. For a full minute Henry made no further move until some inborn instinct told her that it was she who must be in command of the situation. Dimly recalling all that her mother had tried to tell her of this important moment in her life she brought her warm young body close to that of her husband and kissed his cheek.

Not so long afterwards she heard Henry breathing deeply and regularly and knew that he slept. She lay beside him, taut and tearless, knowing that the short time which had elapsed since he had come to her had sealed her fate in so far as marital happiness was concerned. Henry was not impotent but his lovemaking was timid, gentle and somehow pathetic; it aroused in her no passion but a protective spirit which was to stand her in good stead in the years ahead. If she had been asked — as she was to be nearly ten years later — what her sentiments were towards Henry she would have been hard put to answer at this stage except that she knew she must help and protect this kindly man who meant so well but had been so ill-equipped by nature to carry out the high role which destiny had forced upon him. Before she slept at last she had penetrating and blinding insight into the difficult future which lay ahead. What must she do to subjugate that wild and earthy streak which shot through her very being like a fiery flame? It was perhaps as well the Pierre de Brézé had more to do than dance attendance on the forlorn and unhappy Queen of England.

Yet when she rode out from the Palace of Westminster two days later to her coronation in Westminster Abbey nobody could have suspected that she was other than a young woman on whom good fortune smiled. Brought up by her grandmother, who was herself a woman of indomitable courage, while Isabella was holding together the tattered remnants of Anjou during René's prolonged imprisonment Margaret had learnt early that the female sex must find an inner strength on which to build their lives. Not for the fearless queens of Anjou was the cushioned couch or the precious atmosphere of the Courts of Love; life was a question of survival.

That this philosophy included protection of the man to whom they were married seemed natural enough to the old Yolande and Isabella, and Margaret assumed the mantle in the manner born. She had early opportunity for showing her new colours in the ante-room of Westminster Abbey.

Margaret wore a gown of white with a simple coronet of gold set with pearls and other jewels and was well aware of the admiration in the eyes of Suffolk and the ageing Beaufort as she joined the company before entering the chancel for the coronation. She was equally quick to note that Henry bore a slightly dazed air as if the proceedings were in some way proving difficult to manage; she moved to his side without haste.

'My dear,' Henry said, 'you look more beautiful than ever. You know that my prayers will sustain you throughout the service; my only wish is that I might be at your side.'

'Can that not be arranged?'

'My uncle of Beaufort thinks it can but my worthy uncle of Gloucester thinks that it would be out of place for me to be too close.'

So that was it; a minor irritation, maybe, but perhaps typical of the quarrel that Gloucester and Beaufort had waged for almost a quarter of a century. Margaret thought quickly. 'My lords,' she said, impulsively to no one in particular, 'I trust that it will be possible for his grace to be as close to the coronation as ceremony shall allow for I need the comforting presence of my lord to sustain me in my ordeal.'

In the confused conversation which immediately followed Margaret was rewarded with an order from Suffolk to his squire to seek out the Chaplain and place a faldstool in the shadows behind the dais. Henry beamed his pleasure and Margaret chose not to look at either Beaufort or Gloucester. Let them both think that she spoke from her heart.

In the solemn moment when Archbishop Stafford of Canterbury placed the crown upon her head she was aware of Henry in the background and the promises she made were as much for him as herself.

Later, in Westminster Hall, she presided over a great feast at which both the King of Scotland and her own father were represented; from her father's ambassador she learnt that one of his staff brought her letters from Anjou. Her impatience to receive news of her home almost dimmed the brilliance of her day.

It was during the three days of jousting and merry making which followed that Margaret met all the nobles of England and their wives, for the summons to the crowning had been definite and allowed for no excuses. While she watched a tournament in the Abbey court-yard Henry sent a page out of the brocade-hung box in which they sat; the boy returned shortly with two youths, both dark-haired and extremely presentable.

'May I present to you my brothers, Margaret; this is Edmund and this is Jasper

Tudor.' Margaret proffered her cheek and both boys stooped to kiss her in turn. About the same age as they were, she found herself more shy with them than with the older members of Henry's court. They eyed her with blatant curiosity which lacked the admiration always forthcoming from Suffolk or Moleyns or, for that matter, old Beaufort himself. Desperately searching for some common ground on which to speak to them she mentioned the kinship between herself, the King of France and their own mother. She saw at once that she could not have chosen a more unfortunate subject for the boys recoiled from her almost physically as if the loss of Katherine was too close to discuss in polite conversation. Margaret took a deep breath. 'You are fond of the chase?' she asked.

'Very,' Jasper replied quickly.

'Then I hope you will accompany Henry and me when we hunt in the forest around my new manor of Enfield.'

'That will give us great pleasure, ma'am,' Edmund said with a polite bow.

'We'll see how soon it can be arranged.' Indeed, Margaret looked forward to a gallop through open countryside with considerable pleasure for the long progress through France and southern England had been both restrictive and formal. It would be most relaxing to feel the cool breeze blowing through her hair and sink into bed healthily tired.

A particular bout in the lists claimed the attention of the young Tudors and they moved to the side of the box for a better view. René's ambassador came to sit next to Margaret.

'Your mother commissioned me to speak privately with you so that I may report to her on your health and happiness, your grace,' he said in an undertone.

'You may tell my mother that I am very well received and happier than I dared hope. I miss both my father and my mother, but that is only natural and will pass when I have a child to care for and Henry allows me to relieve him of some of the burdens of state.'

The ambassador looked swiftly up into her face but saw nothing but a benign smile for the contestants in the yard below. 'You will see from the letter we have brought that my lord, your father, is most anxious that the peace treaty signed between England and France should be more permanently based. Has anything been mentioned in your presence about the terms of such a treaty?'

Margaret shook her head. 'I have heard nothing but eulogies and marriage settlements since I have been here.'

'Forgive me but his grace, your husband, must be more wealthy than we were led to believe for that collar which you are wearing today, as well as being of exquisite workmanship, must have strained his exchequer to the limits.'

'Do you think so?' Margaret asked, wonderingly, touching the heavy necklace about her throat. 'I think I remember Lady Isabel Grey telling me that it was an old piece belonging to the monarch. No mention was made to me of purchasing such a rich object.'

Nor would it be, the ambassador thought; nor of the probable subject of its redemption from some wealthy money lender. If what Orleans had told them was correct the King of England was hardly less impoverished than his own royal master; such was the cost of waging perpetual war. Peace was a vital necessity and Beaufort, Suffolk and those who supported him must be prevailed upon to consolidate the truce with all speed.

* * *

So successful was this campaign that Suffolk told Henry that he had arranged for a French delegation to come to England in the following July to negotiate a lasting peace; and so well did he put his case that even Gloucester, his most bitter opponent, could find no fault with the arrangements he made. For Suffolk went so far to quiet his critics that he sent orders to the Duke of York in Normandy to fortify the towns of Le Mans and Rouen against seizure by the French. Thus was all suspicion allayed that Suffolk might have traded the jealously guarded French possessions of Maine as the price of purchasing René's daughter for his king.

On the face of it Margaret's reign as queen had begun under the most auspicious circumstances. Suffolk was at the highest peak of his popularity and Beaufort and Gloucester seemed to be reconciled for the present.

Yet, when René wrote to her telling her never to forget her homeland and Anjou's claim to Maine, what could she do other than promise her beloved father that she would do all in her power to see that his lands were restored to him? The world was at her feet and, like a fairy godmother, she had but to wave her wand for her smallest wish to be granted.

She could not have known that the English people felt very strongly indeed about relinquishing land in France for which they had paid dearly in both money and blood for longer than most could remember; and perhaps, even if she had, she still would have wished to please René.

5

'Come in.' Margaret looked up from the letter she was writing to her uncle King Charles of France as Lady Isabel Grey entered her private solar at Westminster to ask if the Marquis of Suffolk might have an audience with his sovereign lady. 'Of course,' Margaret cried gladly. 'Why, my lord, it is an age since we have seen you and enjoyed your lavish hospitality at Wingfield. I shall never forget those evenings when we were surrounded by so many learned men that I felt I must read every book that has ever been written. Is Lady Alice well?'

'I thank you, yes, and sends her most respectful and devoted greetings. I trust that his grace is keeping free from the rheums that are affecting most of his subjects?'

'He is well and is with his chaplain working on a life of St. Jerome at this moment. Shall I send Isabel to request his presence?'

'No,' Suffolk shook his head, 'my business is with you, my lady. I have just received the news that another embassy from France will be arriving here before Christmas and I come to implore you to ask the king to come to a conclusion on the matter of settling the truce.'

'But his grace has already consented to cede Maine as part of the agreement — have I not persuaded him over the past two years that nothing less than giving up this territory will satisfy my uncle of France — what more can we do to convince the delegates?'

'Cardinal Beaufort considers, and I entirely agree with him, that the truce must be extended beyond the date of April next year and that orders should be sent to the Earl of Dorset to surrender at Le Mans as a token of the English intention.'

'But Dorset will surely not agree to that?'

'He might be persuaded.'

'But what of Gloucester?'

'My lord of Gloucester chooses to oppose any measure that the Cardinal or I consider necessary to bring peace to this realm.' Suffolk's voice had a rasping edge to it and Margaret recognised the signs of his growing impatience with the king's uncle. Of late she had heard a great deal from Alice and others of the incompetence of Gloucester and his determination to have his way with Henry. More than once Margaret had caught muttered criticisms of Gloucester's management of the country's finances and knew full well that Suffolk and many others thought the royal duke was enriching himself at the expense of an already impoverished nation. Gloucester had retaliated in the Parliaments which had met during 1445 and 1446 and had heaped abuse on Suffolk, the Cardinal and Edmund, Duke of Beaufort, for their policy in France; his fury growing as the sympathy of the English people supported him.

Margaret, determined to support those who had brought about her marriage, came to detest the king's uncle and Gloucester was now seldom at court.

'Has the Cardinal not spoken with my husband upon the dire necessity of prolonging the peace?'

'My lady, I very much regret that his grace of Beaufort is not as well as he might be; he is a man of many years and has been carried forward by his indomitable spirit but I fear that we shall not have his support for very much longer.'

'If that is the case,' Margaret replied with spirit, 'then I must speak with Henry at the earliest opportunity for this matter has been too long protracted.'

'There is, also,' Suffolk said, seizing the opportunity to further his cause against Gloucester, 'the matter of Duke Humphrey's wife.'

'Eleanor Cobham? What business is my lord of Gloucester forwarding on her behalf? Has not the lady been imprisoned for years?'

'Yes, most certainly; since the day, in fact, when she was found guilty of necromancy and treason. It is apparently the duke's intention that his wife may now be released.'

'For what purpose?' Margaret asked, puzzled. It had never seemed to her that Humphrey lacked for female company and his marriages were not renowned for the happiness which they might have brought him.

'Well,' Suffolk said slowly, 'I think, and so do many others, that my lord of Gloucester wishes to have Eleanor released so that he and she may once more practise their black arts.'

'To what purpose?'

'Against the king's grace,' Suffolk supplied bluntly.

'But that is impossible,' Margaret rounded on Suffolk.

'Not as impossible as you may believe, my lady; it was with treason that Eleanor was charged and she worked for no one else but her husband. You must not forget that Duke Humphrey still remains heir to the English throne.'

Margaret shivered. Could it be that there

was some curse on Henry? Her common sense and intelligence overcame her superstitious fears after a moment or two and she looked at Suffolk squarely.

'I do not think I fear my lord of Gloucester on that score but, in the matter of the French peace, I shall speak immediately with the king. You may safely leave the matter with me; there is nothing I desire more than that our two realms should live in harmony.'

'Nothing gives me more satisfaction than to hear you speak thus upon a subject which is so dear to my heart. England has a champion indeed in you, madam, and Gloucester and York will live to rue the day they opposed our honourable intentions. Will you and his grace do me the honour of coming to my house this evening for supper? I have commissioned some new music to mark the anniversary of your highness's marriage and it would give me great pleasure if you were to hear it tonight.'

'I am pleased to accept your kind invitation,' Margaret said with real sincerity, for, without the occasional visits to those nobles in Suffolk's circle, life would have been tedious in the extreme.

When her most trusted minister had departed Margaret rolled up the letter she was writing to the King of France and sent a page to bring her some mulled wine. She felt cold and uneasy. While she awaited the boy's return she sat by the newly replenished fire and thought over what Suffolk had been saying to her.

She had been sufficiently long in England to assess the existing impasse that existed between the two proud noblemen and gave her entire support to the man who had signed the marriage treaty between herself and Henry. From her waiting women she heard the current rumours of Gloucester's misdemeanours and had developed a very real dislike of the man. This had not been the sole reason for turning against Henry's uncle for she had been quick to discover that her husband hung on his words and had always been ready to take his advice. This did not please Suffolk and his party or Margaret herself for, as time went by and she showed no signs of giving England its long-awaited heir, Humphrey presented a real threat to the succession. It would have been so much easier if Bedford, Henry V's other brother, had lived or produced an heir for he had been selfless in the cause of his country's progress and put everything else in second place.

As for Henry himself Margaret could only regard him with the tolerant and binding affection of a mother for a devoted but slightly backward son; he had no vice in him and intended only the best towards all men. His main interests were the school and college he was building at Eton and Cambridge for impoverished boys and he frequently told Margaret that the nobles of his court should follow his example and keep their minds on things spiritual. There were times when Margaret was in complete agreement with him but she knew that a lasting peace was as necessary to England's future as establishments of learning.

When the wine had warmed her a little she went in search of her husband and did not leave until she had his promise that he would receive the French embassy and give his blessing to an early settlement.

The ambassadors of Charles VII came and went and if Margaret was disappointed that Pierre de Brézé was not of their number but, in the emotional strain of bending English ministers to carry out Henry's wishes, she soon forgot that she had had some kind of day-dream that she might renew her friend-ship with that brilliant and highly attractive officer of the French court. It was one thing to persuade Henry that England should relinquish her hold on territories which rightly belonged to her father or the king of

France but quite another to break the stubborn refusal of his Council to agree. Margaret was in despair by the time the delegation crossed the Channel; a desperation only slightly mollified by the presence of Moleyns and other English ambassadors in the train. What if she should fail England by not producing the heir it so urgently needed and underline her failure by not bringing about the terms of the truce which had been the reason for her marriage? Seventeen is an early age to discover that one's husband is loving but no lover and, into the bargain, is quite contented to permit his wife to shoulder the heavy burdens of state.

Christmas, spent quietly at Shene, did nothing to alleviate her misery, for the festive spirit with which she had tried to imbue the feasts and masques was dimmed by the news that Cardinal Beaufort was failing fast. Henry, who had a deep affection for this half-brother of his grandfather, had passed on this sentiment to Margaret and she was as grieved as he to learn that the autocratic but wise old man was suffering in his palace at Winchester.

Nor was the new year to bring her much comfort. On the day following Epiphany she and Henry rode with a large number of attendants to Westminster; the day was dreary with a biting wind and Margaret huddled into the new fur robe which had been Henry's present to her. She could not help but think of her warm birthplace where the crickets chattered endlessly in the sunny, flower-strewn meadows and tried not to contrast it too nostalgically with the gaunt elms crowned with cawing rooks which bordered their path. She comforted herself throughout the unpleasant journey with the thought of the hot bath and roaring fire which would be prepared for her on arrival at the London palace.

Yet, hardly had she enjoyed the sensuous pleasure of immersing herself in scented water, and had put on clean clothing than Rose, who was acting as her lady-in-waiting because Isabel Grey had gone home to be with her mother and sons over the Christmas celebrations, came to say that Henry requested her immediate presence in his private apartments. Margaret put down the boards, paper and paints with which she had thought to amuse herself during the long evening ahead, and hurried to join her husband.

She found Henry in an extremely agitated condition, with beads of sweat at his temples. 'My lord,' she cried, concern overcoming her usually discreet manner, 'what ails you? You have not taken a chill during that dreadful ride?'

'No, no,' Henry said, brushing aside the suggestion, 'I am rarely ill as you know; this is something of much graver importance than my health. My lord of Suffolk was awaiting our return from Shene and he came at once to me with an urgent request that my uncle of Gloucester should be impeached at the next Parliament — '

'Impeached? On what grounds?'

'His misappropriation of monies granted him for use in the realm and some charge that he has been practising witchcraft.' Henry was obviously bewildered and Margaret went to stand at his side, her hand comfortingly on his shoulder. She was as shocked as Henry but knew that this was not the moment to betray her anxiety.

'If my lord of Suffolk has sufficient evidence to prove that Humphrey of Gloucester is deserving of punishment then he must be brought to trial,' she said slowly. 'Our good friend does not act hastily and has always given us good advice in the past.' She could not say that she had never trusted the king's uncle and was prepared to back the judgement of Suffolk for, although Henry was in agreement with his minister's (and his wife's) plans for prolonging the peace with

81

France, Gloucester was a close blood relation and it was not so long since Henry had been utterly dependent upon him.

'I wish my uncle of Beaufort was here,' Henry said plaintively, 'he always knows just what to do when a crisis occurs.'

'Perhaps we might send a courier to Winchester to ask his opinion.'

Henry shook his head. 'I am afraid no good would come from that because I had word from his chaplain as soon as we arrived to say that he is very weak and stays in his bed most of the time.'

'Then we shall have to trust in my lord of Suffolk,' Margaret said, keeping her voice steady. 'Now, shall I stay with you and play a game of chequers?'

'Yes, yes, if you would be so good.'

On the following morning Suffolk asked if she would receive him and she was closeted with him for an hour while he strode up and down her small parlour ranting at Gloucester. 'That man must go,' he stormed. 'There will be no peace in the realm until he is banished. Do you realise, madam, he sits in that manor of his at Devizes plotting the downfall of your house and mine?'

Once more Margaret shivered. 'You are certain that he intends harm to Henry and to me?'

'I am as sure of that as I am that he would gather an expeditionary force together tomorrow and set out to subjugate France.'

'That must not happen at whatever cost!' Margaret cried. 'Set in motion the necessary measures for calling Parliament together.'

So in the bleakest of weather she and Henry once more took to the roads; this time bound for Bury St. Edmunds where Suffolk had chosen to summon the Parliament. They were accompanied by a huge army of men. When Henry had protested, mildly, that he did not usually need such a protective entourage Suffolk had assured him that he had never before ridden out in such dangerous and uncertain times.

Margaret, flanked on both sides by a stalwart soldier mounted on a sturdy charger, was muffled to the eyes in her furred cloak. Yet, despite this rich protection, she was stiff and frozen with the cold and almost unable to descend from the saddle to rest in Royston and Cambridge. She found the streets of both places surprisingly free from the usual press of citizens gathered to wish their king well.

'Nothing but this damnable cold keeps them from lining the pathways, madam,' Suffolk assured her. 'There are older men among us who say they have never seen such frozen roads or known such cold in their aching bones.'

But Margaret was not convinced that it was only the icy winter which prevented Henry's subjects from cheering him on his way; the faces which had peered out at them from half-shuttered casements and frosted panes had been unsmiling and unfriendly. Had Gloucester more support than she imagined? If this were the case the sooner he was sent packing to some banishment abroad the better for England. With his warlike ideas and dabbling in the occult he was better out of the way.

Soon after their arrival at their residence in the pleasant house close to the Abbey of St. Edmund the Parliament was convened and the question of arranging a meeting in the near future between Henry and Charles of France was discussed. Suffolk lost no time, as Gloucester had not yet made his appearance, in putting his case against the king's uncle. Receiving the support of those nobles who had pitted themselves against the Siberian weather to attend, the King was persuaded to order Gloucester's arrest as soon as he put foot in the town.

For several days it appeared as if Humphrey was ignoring the summons and had been warned to keep within the safety of his Devizes home. However on the morning of the eighteenth of February Suffolk heard through spies he had posted on the road from Newmarket that Gloucester was approaching with only a small band of followers.

'Poor man,' Henry said to Margaret when he was told of the imminent arrival of his uncle. Turning to Sir Thomas Stanley, Controller of his household, he gave orders that Gloucester was to be escorted straight away to his lodgings. 'Let him rest in peace there from this appalling cold.'

Margaret, torn between an unlooked-for pity for the unsuspecting Duke and concern that Henry should not now weaken in the decision which had been made to rid the realm of the troublesome magnate, hurried to her chamber and sent for Suffolk.

'Leave it to me, your grace,' Suffolk assured her, 'I'll not be tardy in imparting to his lordship the real reason for this Parliament. Let him eat his meat in peace and then I'll send Dorset and some of the others to him in North Gate House. Be you so good as to keep the king's grace at his devotions and I'll see to the putting down of this meddling tyrant.'

Margaret went to bed that evening with no further word from Suffolk. The wives of Buckingham and Salisbury spent two or three hours with her before she retired but they spoke of anything but the Parliament and she went to bed in a fervour of impatience to know how Gloucester had taken the news of his arrest.

She had taken but little of her bread and ale to break her fast on the following morning when a lady-in-waiting came to ask if Suffolk might speak with her. Pushing aside her half-eaten food she told the woman to bring him with all haste. 'What news, my lord?'

'Half his household is under arrest and Gloucester himself has been warned that a similar fate awaits him when — ' Suffolk's voice was even but there was a wary, taut look in his face that Margaret had not seen before, — 'he recovers from the effects of the journey. It would seem that he has some ague or such like fever.'

'He was shocked by the charge?'

'Very much so; but it will take more than a notice of impeachment to shake the nerve of his grace, I'm quite sure.'

'Have you eaten?' Margaret asked.

'No, and I'll be glad to drink a warm posset with you, for if the truth be told I cannot remember such a day of cold. The wind bites through even the thickest of clothing and I feel chilled to the marrow.'

Suffolk spent an hour with her before

leaving to visit Henry and then later, with the majority of the household, Margaret went to the Abbey church for the second time that day.

She was glad when it became time to go to bed that night for she had been restless through all the hours of daylight and had been unable to settle to any book or handicraft. Henry spent all his time in prayer with the Abbot while Suffolk and the other nobles attended meetings of the Parliament.

It was Lady Suffolk who awoke Margaret in the morning with the astounding news that Gloucester had been found dead in his bed at the North Gate House where he had been lodged. Alice de la Pole was in a highly excitable state fluctuating between astonishment and a thinly-disguised relief that nature had taken a hand in resolving the difficulties facing Henry and her husband as first minister in the land.

Margaret, confessing to a similar sensation of deliverance, was almost immediately subjected to a violent fit of shivering. Some small warning voice in her most innermost heart told that such expedient deaths came too pat upon their necessity and she recalled with acute anxiety hearing René and her mother talking about friends or enemies of theirs who had met their ends suddenly.

'You are sure,' she asked Alice, in a choked voice, 'that no foul play is suspected?'

'How could you imagine such a thing?' Alice cried.

'Only too easily, unfortunately,' Margaret replied, 'and I fear that I shall not be the only one to put such an assessment upon the death of the king's uncle. Oh, how I wish this had not happened! And in Bury St. Edmunds of all places where the holy martyr is renowned for bringing vengeance upon those who live by the sword.'

Alice regarded her royal mistress with a look of consternation; it was unlike Margaret to be a prophetess of woe and she appeared at this moment to be drained of vitality. 'You are not sickening for a chill, your grace?'

'That could be it,' Margaret said, grasping any explanation for the trembling which afflicted her limbs uncontrollably. 'Would you ask Rose to bring me some mulled wine.'

While Alice bustled out of the room Margaret huddled into her chamber-robe and went to the hearth, kicking the slumbering ashes into reluctant life. She prayed that her misgivings were nothing more than the shock which she had received and that the untimely death of Gloucester would prove as beneficial as it might at first appear. She could not put from her mind the sullen crowds who had watched their progress to Bury and the remembrance that Suffolk had been as often accused of malpractices as had Gloucester. To rid themselves of one enemy in dubious circumstances might be to bring a more formidable antagonist to the fore. 'I must put these foolish fancies out of my mind,' she told herself resolutely, 'and thank God that I have such friends as the Suffolks. I am merely a girl, untried in statecraft as yet, and must be grateful that I have those about me who are wise and strong.'

6

Gloucester's death hung over Margaret like the grey, lowering skies of England throughout the following spring. This was despite the fact that Henry, at Suffolk's instigation, gave her many of his late uncle's estates and from the large income they brought guided her into founding the college at Cambridge which had long been her dream.

Margaret, journeying from the ill-fated Bury St. Edmunds to Canterbury with the king, talked with Andrew Doket, the rector of St. Botolph's in Cambridge who had first mooted the idea of the queen following her husband's example to provide more education for worthy scholars.

'But surely, sir, if I am to interest myself in this college it should have the queen's name mentioned somewhere in its title,' she said, with spirit and a smile which Doket found hard to resist.

'Well, I had intended that the foundation should be called for St. Bernard but I can think of nothing happier than to call the place Queen's College. Particularly, my lady, as you are the first to uphold our ideas.'

'That's settled then,' Margaret cried gaily, clinching the matter by a quick decision which she had learnt was the best method of having her own way. 'And, as you have been so hardworking in the drawing up of the plans, I suggest that we include the name of St. Bernard in the title; how do you think 'Queen's College of St. Mary and St. Bernard' sounds?'

She turned to face the aesthetic man who rode beside her and, when she saw him hesitate for a fraction of a second, quickly added: 'It would not do, I think, to mention earthly queens without including the first lady of heaven so our Lady should precede any other saint.'

'Very well, your grace,' Doket agreed, 'and when once I have been granted the Charter to proceed you and I may speak again, perhaps, about the monies that will be necessary to start building.'

'Oh yes, of course,' Margaret said, with a somewhat vague but extremely graceful wave of her hand. 'And, Mr. Doket, there is that question of my lady-in-waiting's brother who is seeking a living in the diocese of Ely. Is it possible that you can bring some pressure to bear upon the bishop? I should be most grateful for your cooperation.'

'I shall look into the matter as soon as I

return to Cambridge,' Doket told her and went on, politely, to discuss the type of chapel he foresaw for his new college and was rewarded with Margaret's genuine interest. Like many other men and women who came into contact with the queen he was sorry that her undeniable talents were wasted in the dowdy court which it was Henry's pleasure to keep. From what Doket heard, the French kings, if they did squabble among themselves a great deal of their time, were gracious in their living and occupied themselves with providing magnificent houses in which to live. Doket glanced covertly at the queen; it was time she was breeding but there certainly appeared no signs of this highly desirable event as yet. What was Henry doing that he did not provide England with an heir? Was he, perhaps, as monkish as he looked and the queen was forced to live in celibacy? When he considered the matter the scholarly priest thought that Margaret had lost some of the bloom which she had brought with her from Anjou and the eyes which had once flashed with interest and provocation were clouded and faintly ringed with shadows. He made some remark which made the girl laugh and he shrugged away his fancies as idle speculation; women were subject to strange moods.

Gloucester's death was not to be the only one in this year of unease and in April 1447 the aged Cardinal Beaufort breathed his last. Henry, genuinely grieving for the wise old autocrat, refused the income which his grand-uncle had bequeathed him, despite Margaret's pleas, and spent the money on masses for the soul of the departed.

Suffolk was now the greatest magnate in the land and if, occasionally, Richard Duke of York complained in Parliament that Edmund Beaufort had been given precedence over him in France he was promised Ireland in its place. Suffolk assured Margaret that all was proceeding peacefully in the realm now that Gloucester's dissenting voice had been silenced and that England was enjoying a quiet time of prosperity.

Yet Richard of York seemed reluctant to depart for Ireland. Margaret, reared to court intrigue, realised that this could well be connected with the royal duke's standing as the new heir-apparent to the English throne. No one but a fool would depart from his home territory when he might be deprived of what he considered his rightful heritage by a similar act to that which had deprived him of the Captaincy-General of France. Richard, however, when he met her was polite and gracious, full of compliments for her beauty and talents.

It was with Isabel Grey that Margaret discussed the seemingly endless ranks of the powerful families of England. Isobel was very well versed in the complicated structure of the connecting marriages between Neville and Beauchamp, Beaufort and Holland. Seated at an open window on a rare fine summer day she would tell Margaret, who had an insatiable curiosity about other people's marriages and children, about the noble families of England. Margaret liked best to talk about York's family; of all those in the land they gave her most cause for thought.

'You know well enough, my lady, that the duke is a direct descendant of Edward III in the same way as his grace, your husband — ' Isabel said one summer day.

'And there are those who think, as he is an heir of an older son, that he has a prior claim to the throne,' Margaret put in quickly.

'There are those,' Isabel answered with a voice smooth as the velvet dress she was wearing, 'but I am not one of them; I believe that my lord Henry with you as his wife will found a dynasty in every way as distinguished as that handed down to him from Henry IV and his illustrious son. But of York's family, now let me see, there are three sons I am quite sure — '

'Who is their mother?' Margaret interrupted.

'She was a Neville, Cecily, the rose of Raby, the youngest child of that prolific Ralph Neville, first Earl of Westmorland, and his second wife Joan Beaufort.'

'So there is Beaufort blood in that family also,' Margaret cried. 'I had not realised that.'

'A very romantic story, my lady, with a happy ending and one that brought fourteen children into the world. No small number when one considers that the earl already had nine children by his first marriage! There is no doubt, however, which family he preferred for although his first brood inherited his title that was about all they did receive and the Beaufort line took all the honours in the way of great marriages and estates that their mother could obtain for them. The first son, Richard, is the old Earl of Salisbury, warden of the Marches towards Scotland, and it is *his* son who has so recently been appointed to act with him to keep the peace with those troublesome warriors over the border; he is married to Anne of Warwick but is unlikely to succeed to the title for his brother-in-law, who, you remember died so suddenly during that bitter cold of '47, left a little girl to follow him.'

'What is the name of this son?' Margaret asked.

'Richard, like his father; Richard Neville.'

So for the first time Margaret heard of the man with whom her fate was to be intricately bound and against whom she was to struggle to keep the Lancastrian monarch upon his shaky throne; yet at this moment she gave the young man no more than a passing thought and turned to speak again of York's sons. 'Tell me the names and ages of the York boys.'

'There is an Edward I think, about seven or eight years, then a George and an Edmund. I rather think that Edmund is the elder of the last two. I do not know them well but have visited their mother when they have stayed at Sheriff Hutton or Middleham castles.'

'So they are still babies?' Margaret mused. Isabel nodded. 'Then, to put it plainly, they are not much of a threat to our throne.' Margaret made this statement in an expressionless tone which still failed to conceal the anxiety behind the remark.

'No, my lady, if Richard of York were to seek more than his expected inheritance as heir-apparent his offspring are too young to aid him any way.'

'I have heard of great nobles dressing their sons in armour as soon as they can sit a horse,' Margaret said drily, 'but I shall not worry too much on that score just now. In fact, I shall put the matter to the back of my mind and concentrate on the coming mission from my father's court; do you think I might ask my lord husband if I may have a new dress for the occasion?'

'Of course,' Isabel Grey said warmly; 'it is an age since you were fitted for a pretty gown and I am sure his grace would not grudge you an opportunity to look your best for Duke René's ambassadors. I'll send a page at once to bring a silk merchant from Cheapside. What colour will you choose?' Isabel was nothing if not warm hearted and she had a passion for lovely clothes.

'A honey silk, I think,' Margaret said while a faint blush stained her cheeks. 'It was always my favourite colour.' If she had been dragged through the streets on a hurdle she would not have confessed that she was praying that Pierre de Brézé would at last be among those who came to pay her their respects and bring letters and encouragement but there was no denying that it was for him that she wanted to look her best. However sycophantic her courtiers or attentive Suffolk their flattery was nothing when put against the memory of that woefully short time before she had left France as a bride.

So it was that when she awaited the arrival of her father's Constable and Comptroller and any other dignitaries who wished to visit England she wore her new dress and placed the enamelled ring with its seed pearl daisy on the first finger of her left hand. Nor, after four years absence from France, was she to be disappointed this time for when the doors were opened to admit the ambassadors she saw, immediately, that Pierre de Brézé was among them.

Politely acknowledging the homage paid her by all the men of the party she tried to look at Pierre without appearing to favour him. This was more difficult than she had imagined and she had to concentrate to answer the loyal greetings brought to her from her father and mother. Letters, she was told, were carried with them and awaited her pleasure for delivery. Henry, who had come in to the ante chamber leaning on Suffolk's arm, made a short and sincere speech of welcome to the men from France and bade them refresh themselves with the wine proffered by several pages who hovered at the side of the panelled room. The official part of the reception finished, Margaret moved down from the dais and was surrounded with the familiar faces of men who had served her father and mother loyally for many years. She questioned them eagerly, hearing with pleasure that all her family were well and looking forward to having first hand news of her. Margaret was slightly chagrined to discover that Pierre was talking to Henry and Suffolk with an Englishman who had attached himself to their party as they had crossed from Harfleur to Southampton. Hiding her disappointment she rather pointedly turned her back on this group about the dais and animatedly plied the emissaries with questions about the vines of this year and the wine of the previous seasons. Let Pierre ignore her and see if she minded!

He did, all the same, come to take leave of her when the rest departed and the kiss that he implanted upon her hand was neither that of a courtier nor a family friend. Margaret could only wonder at the eccentric behaviour of men and wander back, very disconsolate, to her own apartments overlooking the broad Thames.

She had been there but half an hour, idly taking up and putting down a tapestry which needed repairing, when Rose came to tell her that the Seigneur de Brézé craved an audience with her. Clutching the piece of needlework on her lap as if it were a life line

Margaret composed herself sufficiently to nod her head and tell Rose to admit the gentleman.

'My lord,' she said, looking him straight in the face, 'I am delighted to welcome you to my husband's court.'

'And I am as delighted to be here, your grace,' He knelt, swiftly and with ease, and took her hand.

'You may go, Rose,' Margaret said over his bowed head and held her breath until the door shut behind the girl. The gesture was not lost on Pierre who looked up at her, a half-smile curving his lips. Margaret beckoned him to sit beside her on the wooden settle in front of the open window; he brought several rolls of paper out of the pouch about his waist and presented them to her.

'I had no difficulty in persuading your father's officers to entrust me with these letters; I hope that I am not being presumptuous in coming to your apartments. To tell the truth I very much wanted to see you on your own so that I may have a true picture of what your life is like in England.'

'You know that no one would be more acceptable.'

'No one?'

'No one.'

'Then I shall ask my first question; what have they done to you here that they have robbed you of that marvellous anticipation of life which shone from you at our last meeting? Do not misunderstand me,' he said, hurriedly, 'I do not think, for one moment, that you are less beautiful or appealing than you were then — in fact, if it were possible I should say that you are lovelier than ever; but you have about you an air of wanhope. Can you tell me about it?'

Margaret hesitated; it would be so easy to pour out her troubles to this kindly and so very attractive man but supposing he were to think her forward and brash to speak of such intimate and immensely personal matters? After all, what did she know of him except that he was a lifelong friend of her father's and had pledged himself to help her more than four long years before? While she debated what to say she unconsciously rubbed the ring which he had given her and after a moment or two he took her hand and held it between his own. Immediately she knew a sense of peace and trust almost as if some strength flowed into her, giving her hope and a renewed confidence in her ability.

'Won't you tell me?' he persisted.

'I have spoken to no one of the matter since I have been married,' she said, slowly.

'Then it is something to do with Henry,' he prompted without undue haste.

'Yes.'

'He is not a good husband?'

'Oh, yes, he is good and kind and so saintly.'

'But he does not make you happy?'

Again she hesitated.

'Well, he does not, does he?'

'No.'

'Because he does not make love to you?' Pierre spoke the words without emotion in the French that had been her accustomed tongue since her childhood and she fought a savage desire to throw herself into his arms and cry her heart out on his shoulder. Instead she replied, almost in a whisper. 'For that reason.'

'I was afraid that it was that which caused you so much pain. Look at me, Margaret,' and he tilted her face so that she could do nothing but regard him eye to eye. 'I want you to know this; what has happened is in no way your fault. Henry has always had a reputation for monkish behaviour and when the marriage was first mooted I objected strongly because I believed that the burden Charles and René put upon you was intolerable for you to bear — '

'Did you do that?'

'I did.'

'You understand me so well, don't you? Better than perhaps I understand myself. How I wish that you were here to advise me.'

'My dear, I would not want to be here only to advise you.'

'What would you of me then?'

'Do you not know?'

'Perhaps I do, but I cannot believe it.'

'Will you believe me if I say that Henry may not seek your bed but there is no place in the world where I should rather be. Forget that I am a statesman with a glib tongue and think of me only as a man; I have wanted you since that day when we talked together in Tours. God,' he said with a sudden burst of anger, 'how lightly we play with other people's lives, subjecting them to our will and blindly making the excuse that we do what we do for our countries and peace. Damnation to any peace treaty between England and France which has brought you to this bondage. Forgive me but I am likely to take you into my arms and prove how deeply I mean what I am saying to you.'

Suddenly more adult than he, Margaret leaned towards him and kissed him, gently, upon the mouth. 'Pierre de Brézé,' she said, with dignity and complete sincerity, 'I love you and have done so, I now realise, since that day after my betrothal; to know that you care about my welfare will do much to help me in this difficult situation here. Can I always count upon your support?'

'For ever,' Pierre replied simply.

'Then it will be as if you have taken me to your bed and I have lain within the clasp of your love. You had best go now, for it will be common knowledge that you have come to deliver letters and I would not have ill spoken of us by the court. Do not, I beg, leave for France without a brief word in private; I could not bear to know you had departed without some token of my regard for you.'

7

When Pierre and the other ambassadors had left for France Suffolk encouraged Henry and Margaret to make a progress to the north of their kingdom.

Suffolk, for no reason that Margaret could easily define, seemed irritable and distrait. More than once this man, who had been adviser and friend to her since that time when he had come to France to ask for her hand in marriage for his king, spoke shortly to the docile Henry and answered her own probing questions tersely. Margaret wondered if the fault lay within herself and that with Pierre as her yardstick she now found all other men wanting. She knew this could not be the case when Alice de la Pole let slip that her husband was sleeping badly and had taken to riding off on his most spirited horse, staying away from home for hours at a time.

On the face of it Suffolk certainly had nothing of which to complain for worldly honours had been heaped upon him by the dependent Henry and grateful queen. After the death of old Beaufort he had taken the reins of government more and more into his own hands and if he promoted his friends at the expense of others seemed quite capable of dealing with York's increasingly hot-tempered opposition; he had, after all, been used to Gloucester's hatred for years and apparently enjoyed pitting himself against criticism.

Over the past months Henry, at Margaret's insistence, had seen that Suffolk was suitably rewarded for his untiring support and he had received the earldom of Pembroke, had been made a chamberlain, a constable of Dover and lord warden of the Cinque ports. Now in July, following the long-protracted handing over to the French of Le Mans and the country of Maine, he had been created a duke. It would have appeared that he had everything to make an ambitious man contented.

Almost as they set out for Wingfield, Suffolk's home, where the royal party were to spend two or three nights on their way northward, word came from Normandy via an emissary of Edmund Beaufort (now Duke of Somerset) that the garrison which had been compelled to relinquish command of Le Mans was having difficulty in establishing itself in new quarters.

Suffolk was with Margaret when the ambassadors arrived. 'Tell them to lodge themselves at Pontorson or some town near

106

there,' Suffolk said, testily.

'But, my lord,' Margaret cried immediately, 'those places are too near Brittany! Surely it is unwise to risk offending his grace the Duke of Brittany?'

'His grace will not take offence when he realises our men are merely seeking quarters — '

'You cannot be certain of that; how often in the past, my lord, have the English taken up an innocent bivouac only to invest a neighbouring town in the near future?'

Suffolk eyed his queen with a speculative and swift eye before saying in a controlled voice that he would see to it that a messenger was sent to Brittany with assurances for the duke of the peaceful intention of the English.

'I hope Francis of Brittany believes him,' Margaret said, genuinely anxious that the dearly bought peace should not so soon be violated.

'Have you not always been able to rely upon my judgement?' Suffolk asked her when the emissaries had gone their ways.

'Why, of course, William,' Margaret replied using his first name in a moment of rare intimacy, 'but you must surely understand that I am deeply concerned that nothing should spoil the truce which my marriage bought for my father and his people?'

'I do understand,' Suffolk assured her, 'and if I tell you that the Seigneur de Brézé is in charge of the proceedings on behalf of his grace the King of France will you rest content that there is no threat to the peace?'

Margaret, unable to decide if there were any especial significance intended in what Suffolk was telling her, dug her fingernails into the palms of her hands and murmured that nothing would give her greater confidence in her hopes for the future.

It certainly seemed, as they set out for Suffolk, that she was fussing unduly for Henry was in high spirits and those who went with them appeared in holiday mood. The weather was set fair and cloudless skies favoured their slow passage through Essex to the castle at Wingfield which had once been the manor house of Suffolk's mother's family. Here Suffolk's wife greeted them with unaffected warmth and regaled them with excellent food and bands of well-trained musicians and mummers. Margaret had not enjoyed herself so much since the last time she had visited Alice's home and she left the place sorry that she could think of no other house where they would be received so comfortably. Not for the first time Margaret found herself thinking how wealthy the Suffolks must be that they had such quantities of the richest and rarest food and draped their walls and beds with extravagant and exotic coverings. Did Henry manage his finances so ill that a newly-created duke lived in better style than his monarch?

She was forcibly reminded of her nagging thoughts when, as they passed through a village not far south of Lincoln, a man rushed from a cott and prostrated himself almost beneath the hooves of Henry's horse.

'My lord, your grace, help me!' he cried, as a woman ran from the doorway and stooped to restrain him. 'I am being evicted from my home and my wife and I shall be without shelter or succour. My lord, you are a man of God and I am told you will listen to the likes of me — take pity, do something, for we shall surely die!'

'What's this, what's this?' Henry said, as his horse shied slightly. 'Margaret, what is this man saying? Is someone hurting him?'

Suffolk came hurrying forward and gave curt orders for the supplicant to be forcibly removed from under the feet of the king's mount. He was dragged away but not before Margaret had caught the despairing words: 'Tailboys is a devil — he shall pay for his misdeeds!'

'Pay no heed,' Suffolk soothed the king when later he rejoined them in the van of the party, 'I have found out from neighbours that he is a man given to fits of melancholy and has a wife who is a shrew. It appears he has suffered some imagined slight and hoped to appeal to your authority.'

'Poor man,' Henry said, sighing, 'I shall pray for him tonight.'

If not on her knees Margaret also gave a great deal of restless thought to the incident, remembering that her first reaction had been one of distaste that her passage through the village should have been barred by a meanly dressed fellow with the temerity to plead directly to his king; but during the rest of her journey she had not been able to forget the forlorn look on the man's face and the ragged homespun of his and his wife's clothing. She recalled, also, part of a name and could not form the whole in her wakeful brain when suddenly, thinking of Suffolk's attitude to the affair, it returned to her without effort: Tailboys. She knew it instantly as a squire of Suffolk's who had land somewhere in the neighbourhood of the hospice in which they were now staying; a man who often accompanied her minister when he set about his own affairs and one whom she had not trusted as she did most of William de la Pole's friends and clients. She resolved to speak with Suffolk first thing in the morning and almost at once she slept.

But Suffolk shrugged off the incident, making it plain that he considered it too lowly a concern for his mistress: Margaret persisted with her questioning until Suffolk promised, with poor grace, to look into the affair.

On the following day she had other matters to divert her for a messenger rode at a gallop from Southampton with letters from Edmund Beaufort in Rouen to say that the Duke of Brittany had complained to him about the English soldiers making their headquarters at Pontorson. With difficulty Margaret restrained herself from pointing out that she had been right in her fears about the place and helped Suffolk draft a reply to Beaufort telling him to caution his men to do nothing to violate the truce.

'Are you sure you should not tell them to move further into Normandy?' Margaret asked Suffolk as the two of them gave François de Surienne his final instructions before he left for Beaufort's headquarters. This man, born in France but an old crony of Suffolk's, was often entrusted with delicate missions and was a master in the art of procrastination. He and Suffolk now exchanged glances before Suffolk said, with resolution, that the Bible told one to keep one's goods at peace by strong protection and he was not going against the Holy Word at this moment.

'Your grace,' Surienne said, smoothly, 'there is not a man among us who would violate that treaty which brought you to our shores and you may rely upon me to keep my word.'

'Thank you, sir,' Margaret said, glad to hear this affirmation of Suffolk's constant statements yet still aware of a small, nagging conviction that the two men regarded her as a beautiful asset to their country but only a woman when matters of great moment were discussed. She arose, impatiently, and went to seek Henry. She must persuade him to add his gentle voice to her pleadings.

★ ★ ★

The progress was not as successful as Suffolk had hoped and Henry and Margaret returned earlier than they had planned when, as they lay at Durham, a large party of their escorting army went over the border into Scotland, raiding and pillaging. The Scots, not surprisingly, were deeply angered at this incident in a truce with their old enemy and while everything was done to smooth over the explosive situation which followed Margaret and Henry returned quickly to Shene.

All that autumn Margaret lived through a
time of doubt and unease; she did not know
what she feared or what made her apprehen-
sive but Suffolk could not keep from her the
number of petitions presented by ordinary
folk for the restitution of property filched
from them by marauding bands and greedy
neighbours. It appeared as if a warlike spirit
was abroad which sought outlet in petty
thieving and disregard for human life and
property.

Margaret spent more time than usual with
her little priest, Andrew Doket, attempting to
find additional sources of financing her
college at Cambridge. 'Perhaps if we give our
people better schooling they will forget their
grievances and make themselves prosperous
by legitimate means,' she told him. 'I doubt
it,' Doket replied, 'but at least your friends are
supporting you; I received a large sum from
the Duchess of Beaufort this week and
another from Lady Welles of Bletsoe. You
remember her, I'm sure, as the widowed
mother of the little lady Margaret Beaufort,
the ward of my lord of Suffolk.'

'Was there not some talk of the child being
betrothed to Suffolk's son?'

'There was, but I doubt if it went further

than asking for papal dispensation as they are within the bounds of consanguinity.'

'Alice de la Pole is a cousin of the late Duke of Somerset?'

Doket nodded. 'And the Lady Margaret is an heiress of considerable fortune on both her father and mother's side.'

'She is fortunate,' Margaret laughed, 'and it's a pity she is not older — we might interest her in our schemes but I think eight is a little young for academic pursuits, do you not agree?'

★   ★   ★

Christmas, with presents from Anjou and messengers from Pierre, dispelled Margaret's gloom and she began to look forward to the awakening of spring. Somewhat to her surprise Henry had taken to coming to her bedchamber to sit and talk with her while she broke her fast in the mornings and a new and warmer friendship sprang up between them. Less shy than he had been when they had married he spoke earnestly to her of his deep beliefs and hope of everlasting life.

It was during one of these cosy and intimate breakfasts that the blow fell. Margaret's excitement at hearing from Isabel Grey that messengers had urgent news from

Anjou was shattered when she discovered that her father wrote to apprise her of an unwarranted attack deep into Brittany on the town of Fougères by those very English soldiers she had been promised were solely seeking shelter at Pontorson.

'Henry,' she cried, while her temples throbbed with the enormous sense of disappointment which overwhelmed her, 'send for my lord of Suffolk that we may acquaint him with this — this insane breach of the peace.'

She strode backwards and forwards in her bedchamber, clad only in her velvet chamber robe, waving aside Isabel's plea to dress, her temper rising.

Suffolk did not appear as quickly as her fury demanded and she sent two pages to seek him out in his lodgings in the Greenwich Palace where the court was to spend Easter. When he arrived, calm and collected, she turned on him with such venom that Henry, Isabel and Rose were amazed. 'My lord, is it not sufficient that our soldiery is unable to restrain itself from crossing the borders into Scotland that it must now violate the lands of Brittany? Did I not warn you that this very thing would happen if our men were not withdrawn? Is Beaufort so weak a leader that he cannot control the men under his command?'

'I do not think, madam, that there is any question of Beaufort being other than in complete control; in fact, he has furthered our cause by the acquisition of a vast amount of treasure which was being hoarded in Fougeres,' Suffolk said, with maddening composure.

'You cannot mean that you condone this shameful act?' Margaret came close to Suffolk, her eyes bright with her anger; she sensed, rather than saw, Henry move, deprecatingly, from his chair in an effort to act as peacemaker but she had no intention of stopping now she had begun. Her whole future had been staked on this peace and here was the man who had done more than any other to further her marriage calmly stating that he did not think the raid was a bad idea.

'We are a long way away, your grace, and do not know the true circumstances — '

'The attack was unprovoked; my father says so.'

'And you believe him?'

'Implicitly. Send word at once to France, to Rouen, that we apologise for this incident and we shall see that it is never repeated.' Her voice was cold and had a haughty edge which Suffolk had never heard before. 'You do not understand, my lord of Suffolk, what hell hounds have been unleashed this day. I pray to God that we may be spared the holocaust which will inevitably follow. You may go.'

She turned on her slippered heel and went into the tiring room. In the justifiable anger which possessed her she would gladly have given orders for her baggage to be packed and made ready for departure. It would be better to rot in Anjou than live here under a cloud of shame.

8

Margaret, Henry and their court moved about the countryside during the following spring and early summer and one fine June morning were together in the king's private solar at his castle in Winchester.

'But why is there no money with which to pay the Duke of Buckingham?' Margaret demanded of Henry as she examined a roll from the table at which he was working.

'You know well enough that we are being pressed on all sides to refund monies that we have borrowed from time to time and there just is nothing left to send to Buckingham in Calais.' Henry replied in his usual soft and gentle voice.

Exasperated, Margaret almost shouted that if they were to lose Calais as they had so many of their possessions in France during the last four months they might as well pull out the English armies and be contented to remain an isolated island. 'Surely you cannot be content to allow all that your father and his forebears gained to slip away from us? Tax the people more heavily than the one-fifteenth that is normally levied in time of war

118

and strengthen the garrisons!'

'But you are forgetting, my dear, that we are not at war and so therefore are unable to take any money from our subjects.'

'We are being forced to retreat on all sides which comes to the same thing,' Margaret retorted. Her face was pale and she was suffering with one of the headaches which had become part of the daily pattern of her life.

Since the graceless François de Surienne had returned to France and launched his highly successful attack upon Fougères Margaret had known no peace of mind. More aware than Henry of the changes of loyalty which confronted weak monarchies she had lived in dread since the outbreak of hostilities between France and her newly adopted country. She did not need Isabel Grey or the faithful Rose to bring her tidings of scurrilous pamphlets and ribald verses in which Suffolk and she were accused of selling England to their French enemies; she had seen the genuine dislike on the withdrawn faces of her husband's people as they had made their way about the countryside during this spring of 1449. In despair she had written to Pierre telling him of her fears and had been only slightly reassured by his comforting reply that he would do all in his power to prevent

Charles of France actually declaring war against her country. If this last catastrophe were to overtake the ministers of the crown her own growing unpopularity would be unbearable. A barren queen was bad enough but one from the ranks of a declared and long-hated foe was anathema.

Margaret was about to summon a clerk from the Comptroller's office when Suffolk was announced. He also was haggard but he greeted his sovereigns with deference and accepted a beaker of wine.

'You have news for us, my lord?' Margaret asked.

'Despatches from Beaufort at Rouen,' Suffolk replied without haste.

'Good news or ill?' Margaret asked, sharply.

'It is difficult to know for certain but he appears to be asking for reinforcements.'

'Why?'

'He considers it to be necessary.'

'Nothing would be necessary, my lord duke, if Fougères had been restored to its rightful owners.' She had never forgiven Suffolk for refusing to call off the English army and restore the booty which had been taken in the raid and her voice was cold. Suffolk heard her in silence, making no effort to justify his fateful decision. Time, he was sure, would show that he had been right and this chit of a handsome girl was not going to provoke him to wrath; he had sufficient of that from York's allies. What a pity that Lord Cromwell and the others could not be sent packing with their ringleader to keep down the recalcitrant Irish; so many problems would be solved in this way.

'You are in agreement that we should send aid to the Duke of Somerset?' Suffolk asked Henry after a somewhat painful minute in which nobody spoke.

'Of course, of course, dear soul; send him what troops we can muster; we cannot afford to lose the Staple.'

'With what shall we pay them?' Margaret enquired acidly. 'Promises of future prosperity or honours and preferments?'

Disgusted with her own ill-grace and helplessness she bade her husband and Suffolk good morning and went out of the room.

In July Charles of France finally declared war against England and Margaret was plunged into the depths of despair. She knew she had Pierre to thank that hostilities had for so long been on an unofficial basis but this formal declaration was a personal death knell.

By October most of Normandy had been regained by the French with Rouen in their hands and Beaufort forced to retreat to the coast. The Queen of England found herself caught in a network of divided loyalties. Many times she wished that she might die of the plague which had been rampant during the past winter and so finish the misery which had become her existence.

'What will become of us?' she asked Isabel one evening in November when they sat with some of her other ladies before a fire in her apartments at Westminster.

'Why, your grace, what makes you ask that question?' Isabel replied, her tranquil face mirroring her genuine surprise.

'You have heard, as often as I, how Suffolk is blamed for all the misfortunes that have befallen us. Do you not think those who have lost loved ones or those who have had their livelihood torn away will want retribution?'

'They may well do so, my lady, but how will that effect you?'

'Suffolk has been our most trusted minister and to peers and Commons alike it will appear that what he has done he has done at our bidding — as indeed he so often has. I am unpopular enough — yes, it is true,' Margaret said quickly as her waiting women gasped and began to protest, 'I am unpopular as a French woman who came here without a dowry, and to this will be added my friendship for a man who has allowed his country to become involved in an expensive war which we are losing. Englishmen, I have discovered, hate being taxed but they hate being beaten even more. I fear that I shall be an outcast.'

'That cannot be so,' cried the wife of Edmund Beaufort. 'You know, madam, that you have friends throughout the land.'

'Yes, I have friends; good and trusted and I thank God for them. Nevertheless I have enemies who would gladly see me brought down; you must never overlook the fact that I am blamed for the ceding of Maine.'

Her ladies did their best to assure Margaret of their loyalty and while Isabel sent a page for wine and marzipan cakes Rose took up a lute and began to sing.

Yet on the following day she had a disturbing conversation with William Booth, her chancellor.

It was a chill November day and the marshes and inland pools surrounding the palace of Westminster were overhung with a wreathing mist which penetrated the very corridors of the place. Margaret found it difficult to warm herself and even a quick walk within the shelter of the privy garden failed to arouse her circulation. She was still wrapped in her outdoor mantle when Booth was admitted.

'Good day, Master Booth, I have sent for mulled wine which might serve to take some of this ague-infested damp from our limbs. Are you well?'

'I am, your grace, but I fear that I have news to impart which grieves me in the telling.' He hesitated, his sympathy going out to the girl whose eyes widened at his words.

'What is this, Master Booth, speak quickly — it is not my lord the king?'

'Oh, no, madam, I left your husband well and contented enough. The news I have for you is of the resignation of the Lord Treasurer, a man we can ill afford to lose at this moment.'

'Bishop Lumley? Resigned? I can hardly believe it, what reason does he give?'

'Ill-health, madam.'

'But you do not believe him?'

Booth could say nothing but 'no'. This girl was too astute for lies.

'Tell me why he chooses to desert us.'

'When Parliament meets two days from now he thinks, as do others, that my lord of Suffolk will be brought to defend himself against many charges and he wishes to have no part in the matter.'

Steadying her voice and clasping her hands

together in her lap Margaret said: 'But this Parliament has been called to vote more money to supply our troops in Normandy.'

'Yes, but the opportunity will be used to bring charges of mismanagement against the duke.'

'He is not alone in the disasters which have overtaken us in Normandy; others must share the blame. My lord of Suffolk has served his country for years both in France as a soldier and lately in high office. What are his faults beyond being unable to wage successful war? Surely if we find him the money — and find it we must — all will be forgiven and forgotten?'

Booth hesitated.

'There are other reasons for complaint?' Margaret's voice was taut, constrained.

'Yes,' Booth agreed with reluctance, 'there are.'

'Tell me what they are.'

'I must tell you first that the crown's revenue is in a sorry state; worse than it has ever been before.'

'What does that mean? I know, only too well, that we are always in debt.'

'That debt now amounts to more than three hundred thousand pounds.'

'We shall never be able to repay such an enormous sum,' Margaret cried. 'How was it

125

allowed to become so large?'

'My dear lady, this is the crux of the quarrel that Buckingham, Cromwell and the Commons have with the Duke of Suffolk; they feel, perhaps, that he has not guided the king wisely in the matter of expenditure.'

Margaret was silent for a moment as pictures of the luxurious manors at Wingfield and Ewelme belonging to Suffolk came into her mind. Before she could bridle her tongue she found herself asking: 'And the lords and Commons think that my lord of Suffolk has feathered his own nest at our expense?'

Booth shifted uncomfortably, his pleasant, round face portraying his dislike of the scene he was now called upon to play. Yet, even in his disquiet, he was able to admire the queen for her plain speaking. What a consort she would have made for a strong king and how callously had Suffolk used her to further his own ends. He found himself angry at the waste of her talents and beauty.

When he left her more than an hour later Margaret sat in the fading light of the Winter afternoon staring through the diamond-paned window until she began to cry. Not the tears of sorrow but the dry sobs of hopeless frustration that wracked her chest and left her weak. Rose cried out in alarm when she entered the room and found her mistress slumped in her chair. 'Master Booth told me you did not wish to be disturbed but I could not let you stay alone in the darkness. Shall I light the tapers?'

'Please do,' Margaret said, 'for I fear that more than hobgoblins lurk in the corners of this room.'

★ ★ ★

When Parliament assembled on the sixth of November it was soon obvious that what Booth had predicted concerning Suffolk was right and that his fellow peers were taking him to task on as many counts as they could muster; to underline their complaints against the first minister in the land they made it absolutely plain that he should answer the indictment made against him by the Commons.

'This is intolerable!' Suffolk blurted out to Margaret when he came to pay his respects to her one evening towards the end of November. 'I'm harried from morning until night with: 'What have you done with this sum of money and why did you not do this or that when you first had news of the taking of Fougéres?' I think this country and all its little commoners have run mad; have they forgotten that I campaigned alongside of them in France for fifteen years?'

'I do not suppose so, my lord,' Margaret replied, soothingly, 'but the English are an obstinate race, as I have found, and once they have taken up a subject they do not easily put it down.'

'That is so and it makes for qualities which I admire, but what business is it of theirs what became of the spoils we captured at Fougéres?'

Margaret looked at him, bravely holding up her chin and compelling him to meet her gaze. 'What did become of the money?'

'It went to pay the army, madam, who had received no wages for a year.'

'Very opportune, my lord, and am I not right in thinking that when François de Surienne discovered that he was not to receive the reward that had been promised him he took himself back to Aragon, to his old master?'

'I do not know what you mean, your grace,' Suffolk replied suavely.

'I think you do, sir.' Margaret picked up the little silver bell on the table beside her and when Rose came to ask her bidding she told her that my lord of Suffolk was leaving. 'Goodnight, my lord,' she said, 'I am quite sure that when you face your critics in the Commons you will acquit yourself well; truth will out, so they say, and you should have nothing to fear.'

This might well have been the case had not friends of Suffolk's tried to murder Lord Cromwell, York's friend, in an affray at the door of the Star Chamber. Tailboys was the ringleader of these desperadoes and no one could be certain if he acted solely on his own initiative in seeking to kill the man who had instigated the Commons in their accusation of Suffolk. Whoever was behind the cowardly act Tailboys was committed to the Tower where it was soon rumoured that, under Suffolk's protection and the king's orders, he was treated with every kindness and would soon be released.

Lord Cromwell found this intolerable; narrowly escaping death he had expected that Tailboys would be imprisoned or fined. He brought an action against his would-be murderer and had the satisfaction of receiving damages and the imprisonment of Tailboys in a London gaol.

Margaret occupied herself writing long and frantic letters to her father and Pierre for guidance. Henry seemed bewildered by the turn of events and asked plaintively for Suffolk. 'Why is William so unhappy?' he asked Margaret two or three times a day. Patiently she would explain the unhappy situation of Henry's chief minister and would see her husband shake his head and then fall on his knees at a prie-dieu to pray for the safety of his most trusted friend.

It seemed as if Parliament would sit for ever but at last it rose so that the members could go home to their families for Christmas.

'So we have come through that ordeal,' Margaret said to Booth when he brought her some household accounts.

'Yes, but I fear it is only a temporary respite, your grace; when they return in January they will have fresh ammunition for their guns; Tailboy's unwarranted attack upon the Lord Cromwell was the most foolish act that any friend of Suffolk's could have attempted.'

'You do not think Tailboys might have been prompted by anyone?'

'Only if the prompter desired to commit suicide, your grace,' Booth replied evenly.

Margaret shuddered. Despite the wearisome months which had preceded this Parliament she realised that Suffolk was the most powerful friend that she and Henry possessed and if he were to die she would be hard put to find a man who had their interests at heart. She knew, only too well, that he made mistakes and had discovered his greedy accumulation of personal fortune with regret but he was a well-tried supporter and could be relied upon for encouragement and entertaining hospitality.

Christmas was spent very quietly at Windsor. This was Henry's birthplace and he was always happy in the old castle for he could walk daily to his new school at Eton. Margaret went with him on the day before Epiphany to distribute largess to the masons and labourers who were laying the foundations of the choir for the magnificent church which would be the crowning glory of the building.

Henry walked ahead with the surveyor to the works and his young half-brothers Edmund and Jasper Tudor accompanied Margaret. She had enjoyed their young company during Christmas, finding their gaiety and lively enthusiasm a refreshing change from the misery of the past weeks. With them she had ridden in Windsor forest and hunted the spotted deer. Both young men were dark and good looking, Edmund quieter than Jasper who was an enormous favourite of the women of the court from still-room maid to lady of the bed-chamber. Half-French as they were, they spoke to her in her own tongue; a gesture which she realised they made to please her.

'Have you ever heard the story of Henry's birth in Windsor?' Jasper asked.

'You cannot tell her grace about that!' Edmund interpolated quickly.

'Why on earth not?' Jasper laughed. 'Our brother is in excellent health and married to the prettiest girl in the kingdom; what possible reason could there be for truth in the old legend?'

'It does not do to tempt providence,' Edmund replied quietly.

'What *is* this?' Margaret asked, intrigued.

'Oh, well, if Edmund thinks I am being stupid — '

'I am sure you are not — and besides, you have aroused my curiosity. Tell me about Henry.'

'Well,' Jasper began lamely, 'when Henry's father returned to fight in France before his birth he had a dream in which he was told that if an heir was born in Windsor it would be the worse for the child. The king thereupon wrote with all haste to Katherine, his wife and later our mother, telling her to stay away from here when it came near her time of delivery. Unfortunately her pains started early and she was forced to remain until Henry was born.' Jasper finished his story in a rush and went on hurriedly, 'Anyone can see, with half an eye, that Henry

132

has never looked better and is completely happy wedded to you.'

'So don't think any more of the fairy-story, my lady,' Edmund put in, 'and if Jasper tries to tell you any others like it, box his ears! Tell me, have you heard that the young scally-wag has organised a mummers' play for this evening?'

'No, that sounds a good idea; are you both taking part?'

'Indeed we are and we shall expect you to bang the table in loud applause at our efforts. Will you forgive me for speaking out of turn if our playing is a success?'

'You are forgiven already,' Margaret said, smiling; 'now let's hurry home and warm ourselves with a hot posset in front of a roaring fire.'

★ ★ ★

Two days later Henry and Margaret learnt that Bishop Moleyns, Keeper of the Privy Seal, had been murdered at Portsmouth by some discontented sailors whom he had travelled south to pay. Booth told the astonished queen that the bishop had endeavoured to make the men accept less than they were expecting and they had turned on him and killed him in cold blood.

133

'Why did he try to make the men take lower wages?' Margaret demanded.

'I do not know, in truth, madam,' Booth said slowly, shaking his head in bewilderment. 'By what I have heard reported the men believed he was trying to keep some of their monies for himself.'

'Ah,' Margaret said with a slow exhalation of breath, 'is the world run mad that it has become covetous for riches?'

'God only knows, lady, and He must regard us with distaste, I fear.'

'Did the bishop not defend himself? Or did no one go to his aid?'

'Apparently not and as he lay dying he called upon my lord of Suffolk; some said calling curses upon his head.'

'Master Booth, if that be true, we can number the days that the duke will remain in our service for his foes will hound him from our side, inexorably; and then what will become of us? I confess I am very much afraid.'

9

Margaret's fears were more than justified. The court returned to Westminster and Parliament reassembled, now determined to rid the country of Suffolk and his evil influences.

On the twenty second day of January Suffolk, in the presence of the lords and Henry who sat on his throne in the council chamber, petitioned the king that he might be permitted to clear himself of all the charges which the words of the dying Moleyns had laid upon him.

'My liege lord,' he pleaded, kneeling at the steps of the dais, 'do not forget that I have been a loyal and faithful servant all the days of my life; my father and four of my brothers died in the service of your father at Agincourt and later. How can I be this traitor that my foes would have you believe? Whatever my faults — and I am but human — I have never been unfaithful to you.'

'Do not listen, sire,' Cromwell shouted, 'he is in the pay of the King of France and thinks nothing save lining his own pocket.'

'You are too hasty, my lord Cromwell, the

duke has always been a good friend to me and loyal to this our country. I shall hear no more of this matter today.'

'But, your grace — ' Ralph Cromwell protested.

'Lord Cromwell,' the Chancellor said, 'his grace has heard your case and considers there is an end to the matter.'

Several of the peers, including Lord Welles, Lord Willoughby and the youthful Earl of Warwick stood up protesting that the hearing had only just begun and no case had been put forward. 'Then that is the finish,' Henry said, with more resolution than was usual. He also rose from his throne and made his way out of the chamber.

Once he had departed the lords pushed and jostled their way into the palace yard, dividing themselves into groups and arguing in loud voices.

Most of this scene was related to Margaret by Booth when she returned from riding out to the village of Chelsea with the young Tudors, who had been knighted by their half-brother during the Christmas recess at Windsor, but were not eligible to be summoned to Parliament.

'So William has escaped,' she said with great relief.

Booth eyed her soberly. 'I should not like to

say that, madam, but at least while his adversaries go off to find further cause to indict charges against him he is given an opportunity to work upon his defence.'

Yet, however Suffolk strove to prove his innocence, his efforts were in vain. The Commons sent their Speaker to the Lord Chancellor to tell him that they believed that Suffolk was so much in the pay of the French that he had fortified the castle of Wellingford in readiness to launch an attack upon his fellow countryman. This firebrand was sufficient to light the smouldering bonfire against the ageing statesman and Suffolk was committed to the Tower.

Margaret found herself unable to eat. Not only was she grieved for the man who had helped her so much in the past but she was frightened for her own position in a near penniless court with no ally to back her weak and gentle husband. Where now could she look for aid? Those lords who strove to bring Suffolk down were not likely to be her friends.

On the seventh day of February Suffolk was brought from the Tower to hear the charges laid against him when all his acts were described as treasonable. A month later he was officially tried by his peers in the council chamber: here it was useless for him to protest that he was still loyal and had had no ulterior motive of hoping to gain the throne for himself by marrying his son John to little Margaret Beaufort. In an atmosphere highly charged with emotional issues his blood was demanded as a sacrifice; his enemies intended that it should be spilt.

Henry tried, weakly, to save his favourite by admitting that Suffolk was probably at fault on some accounts and that five years in banishment would cure his presumption.

Exalted with this royal protection Suffolk left Westminister for his home at Wingfield. As he rode through the gateway of the palace an angry London mob seethed out from the vicinity of St. Giles church and succeeded in unhorsing the man whom they blamed for the reverses in France and the general malaise which appeared to be gripping the country. Suffolk escaped only by the quick action of one of his grooms who pulled him from his horse and ran with him up a dark alley. Guards were summoned from the palace and after a noisy hour the crowd dispersed. But his enemies were determined and the tragedy reached its inevitable climax when Suffolk headed towards Flanders and banishment. The pinnace on which he was making the sea crossing was intercepted by a belligerent band who dragged the duke on board their boat and beheaded him with a rusty and none too sharp sword.

Edmund and Jasper Tudor heard the news as they came into the castle of Leicester where the court was assembling for the next session of Parliament.

'Good grief,' Jasper said, 'the man may have been grasping but he surely did not deserve such a death; did I hear right that his body was left upon the sands close to Dover and that his head has been sent to our brother?'

Edmund shuddered, his sensitive face registering his dismay. 'I am sure that what you heard about the head was an exaggeration although nothing would surprise me. What concerns me is how the queen will take this.'

'You do not believe that foolish talk that she was in love with Suffolk?' Jasper asked, incredulous.

'No, of course not, but she has few friends upon whom she may rely and, even if she did not always see eye to eye with William de la Pole, at least he was a faithful servant and counsellor. To whom will she look now?'

'She has Lord Say and Viscount Beaumont.'

'They are not of the same calibre as Suffolk. I wish that you and I were older and had more standing so that we might aid Henry and his wife; he has done so much for us that we are greatly in his debt.'

'We are learning much while we are at court and we must train ourselves to be of help to our brother. Do you think that Edmund Beaufort is loyal to the queen?'

'I am sure he is but he has his hands full with trying to retain what small possessions we have in France.'

'What a pity that the Duke of York was such a dedicated foe of Suffolk's, for if he had not been perhaps he would have been more devoted to the queen.'

'When he knows that Suffolk has finally been removed from influencing Henry and the queen he may ask to be replaced in Ireland and come to support his cousin.'

'Who knows,' Jasper said, as they came to the door leading into Margaret's apartments. 'But at least we can lessen her burden at the moment by breaking the news of Suffolk's death as easily as possible. Shall we do it straight away and have done with it?'

Margaret took the news of Suffolk's death so calmly that the Tudor brothers were amazed at her dignity and selfpossession. They would have been less surprised if they had been with her in her apartments during the evening after they had spoken with her.

Rose was hard put to know how best to deal with her distraught mistress. Had it been one of her own sisters she would have administered a swift slap to Margaret's face and hoped the shock would have calmed her. As it was she stood hopelessly at the young queen's side murmuring entirely ineffectual words of sympathy and encouragement.

'What shall I do?' Margaret wailed for the tenth time. 'Who will now guide us? Who will speak with our voice to these hostile lords and their upstart Commons?'

'The people love you, madam,' Rose comforted.

'They do not — they hate me because I am barren and a Frenchwoman. I wish that I had never come to England and had stayed beside the peaceful Loire.'

Rose seized upon this reference to her homeland and suggested that perhaps there might be someone to whom Margaret could appeal in Anjou. 'Your father, why do you not write to him?'

'What can he do? He is tired of making wars and fighting other people's battles. I expect that he is tired of hearing of my failures — '

'That cannot be true, my lady, for he writes to you constantly and you have never told me that he is out of patience.' Rose cast

141

desperately in her mind for likely helpers in this crisis. 'Shall I send for Sir Edmund or his brother? They are — '

'Certainly not,' Margaret said, with returning spirit, 'I would not have them know that I am brought to this level.' She stood up from the hard stool on which she had earlier slumped, and began pacing the floor. Rose found herself thinking of the caged tigers she had watched in the menagerie at the Tower; there was something very similar between the queen's restless, desperate strength and those unwillingly pent creatures. Not for the first time the waiting woman felt great sympathy for her mistress and almost without knowing that she did so she prayed for help.

It arrived most unexpectedly in the form of a page who came from the king begging his wife to come to him in his hour of sorrow. The queen's grief turned to towering rage as she rounded on the hapless boy.

'Who broke the news to his grace? Did I not give the strictest orders that it should be I who acquainted him with this foul murder? Who dared to disobey me? What fool thought he knew better than I? Rose, bring me a cloak and come with me to the king's apartments. I'll have whoever caused this effrontery confined in the Marshalsea.'

Margaret found Henry sitting at his

working table, unopened rolls of parchment upon it, his face waxen and his eyes clouded with suffering. She forgot her own misery and fell on her knees beside her husband cradling his head against her bosom. 'Send for Sir Edmund and Sir Jasper,' she said crisply to the gawping page, 'and make haste about it.'

'Oh, my dear, what is the world coming to?' Henry whimpered. 'Moleyns first and now William. Are we such tyrants that our people distrust us and wish us dead?'

'No, of course not; there are evil men about who envy the powerful.'

'If they would only heed the Holy Book,' Henry said.

'If only they would,' Margaret replied in the absentminded voice in which she would have comforted a suffering child, 'but they do not and we shall have to find other means of ensuring a peaceful future.'

'You want that, don't you dearest Margaret?'

'More than anything.'

But there seemed little chance of realising this wish for although Parliament in this session voted the king a much-needed subsidy it had hardly done so when messengers came post haste from London with the news that large disturbances had broken out in Kent. Lord Say quickly told the king that this was no new occurrence and one that could easily be dealt with by a strong contingent of armed men.

'On the contrary,' Sir Humphrey Stafford, who had acted as the bearer of these fateful tidings, interrupted, 'this is not a case of men taking the law into their own hands but appears to be a quiet gathering together of an army who are slowly making their way towards London.'

'Then we must surely stop them,' cried Jasper Tudor, who hastily retreated into a corner, his face bright scarlet, when his older brother glared at him.

'What do you think we should do?' Henry asked Archbishop Kemp. The priest hesitated before replying that it might be advisable to wait and see if the trouble blew over.

Lord Say was heard to mutter that this was the type of advice that might be expected from a namby-pamby cleric and it was a great pity that old Cardinal Beaufort was dead as he would have lost no time in jumping into his war saddle and riding straight down to the Kentish countryside.

After much debate, when tempers frayed and the lords shouted at one another in most unparliamentary behaviour, it was decided that the Council should be dissolved and the king go south to meet whatever threat there might be to the peace of his realm.

Margaret prayed as they jogged through the tranquil lanes, where honeysuckle mingled its sweet scent with that of the dog rose, that on reaching their destination of St. John's Priory in Clerkenwell within the City of London they might discover that the rumour was illfounded and the massed men nothing more than one of the tyrannous bands of outlaws who nowadays too frequently preyed upon their neighbours. Henry had hardly had time to recover from the shock of Suffolk's assassination before this fresh anxiety was laid upon his shoulders and he looked more withdrawn and pale than usual. He had also been most disappointed that many of the lords who had been present at Leicester had failed to accompany him to the capital.

As they rode into the cobbled yard of a hospice near Godmanchester where they were to rest for the night he referred for perhaps the fourth time to his regret that more of his peers were not lending him their aid. 'That young Warwick, who turned out with such a fine showing of scarlet-clad followers to attend the Council, why is he not with us? He seems a fine young man and commands respect among his people.'

'He must be very wealthy,' Margaret said with the practical assessment of character which lately seemed to supersede any other.

'Aye,' Henry told her as a squire helped him alight, 'his wife brought him a great many estates and no doubt when old Salisbury dies he will come into a great many more.'

'We should cultivate his friendship,' Margaret replied, 'for now we have enough money, so Booth tells me, to scrape through until Christmas but after that we shall be looking for succour once more.'

Ignoring this worldly talk Henry went on: 'Warwick is about your age, dearest, and his wife is a pretty young thing; they would make good companions for you, would they not?'

'I have friends enough,' Margaret replied shortly and allowed herself the rare indulgence of thinking of Pierre for a moment or two. She had written to tell him of Suffolk's death and as yet had no reply; communication between them had been restricted since the outbreak of hostilities but Pierre had trusted messengers and she hoped one of them would succeed in coming to her soon.

If she had been asked about her personal feelings and emotions during this time she would have been at a loss to answer with truth for she was so occupied with bolstering Henry that every other need was submerged. She realised, as she gradually assumed more

146

of the supporting role which had been played by Suffolk, that she loved her gentle husband in a dedicated and protective manner. Henry, bereft from babyhood of his father and brought up largely in the hands of tutors away from his widowed mother, was in constant need of reassurance and guidance. He would have been quite content to sit with his priests and talk of spiritual matters all day long and Margaret had to be firm with him so that he attended the councils in which she and his ministers took decisions. Apart from his devotions the only matter in which he was obdurate was his continued protection of his young half-brothers and their sister who remained in the care of the nuns to whom she had been committed during the last days of Katherine de Valois. It was as if he tried to make up to his dead mother for the injustices which had been wrought upon her by Humphrey of Gloucester; he was certainly rewarded by the loyalty and affection given him by both Edmund and Jasper Tudor.

★ ★ ★

When the royal party with its supporting army of twenty thousand armed men rode into London they were greeted by an excited and grateful Mayor and Common Council. It was obvious by the glowing speeches which were made that Henry was seen as a worthy successor of his warlike father. Once again the spirit of Agincourt walked proudly through the narrow alleyways and Henry's soldiers drank its health in mighty fashion in the hundreds of inns about the city.

Soon spies brought in the welcome news that the Kentish rebels had withdrawn to Sevenoaks from a camp they had pitched at Blackheath.

'Praise be,' Henry said thankfully as they ate a very good meal at the invitation of the Prior. 'Perhaps we shall now be able to depart and continue our progress.'

'Oh, surely not, your grace,' Lord Say cried, 'this is the time to show you are determined to have no more of these insurrections.'

'But we are dealing with just another discontented band who have nothing better to do at the moment than cause trouble.'

'That is not the case,' Lord Beauchamp stated, shaking his head and frowning anxiously. 'I have it on the best authority that this man Jack Cade has a following of many thousands and it is made up of gentlemen, farmers and honest tradespeople; there are few outlaws with them.'

'Then what are their grievances?' Margaret

asked, keeping her voice even.

Beauchamp glanced about the room, uneasily. 'They have a charter, madam, which protests strongly about the state of the country — '

'In what way?'

'The heavy taxation, the unfairness of magistrates who favour the rich and the powerful and the insecurity of life in which neither a man's life nor his possessions are secure. They think that we, the lords, are not concerned with their problems and seek only to line our own pockets.'

Heated discussion broke out in the stuffy parlour and the company did not rise until the lords had made the decision to ride out and confront the malcontents.

Margaret, who was greatly disturbed at the outcome of such a confrontation, persuaded Henry to remain in the priory for two further days until all his troops were ready to set out for Blackheath. There, in the camp so recently abandoned by the Cade followers, Henry and she made a temporary home in a striped pavilion and it was here that she first learnt that Cade, who called himself Mortimer, might indeed be an adherent of the Duke of York who claimed his descent from Edward III through the Mortimer family. It was Jasper who brought this piece of very interesting information and warned his sister-in-law that there might be deeper implications than just oppressed commoners to combat.

Lord Say and the other nobles sent out a forward party on the following morning to confront the Captain of Kent, as he was styling himself, and both Sir Humphrey and Sir William Stafford who led the soldiers were killed with many of their men. This most unexpected calamity spread disaffection among the royal troops, who were now in no great stomach for a fight despite the enthusiasm of the London Mayor and Council and the unfortunate Lord Say was committed to the Tower in an effort to appease them.

Margaret, bearing in mind what Jasper had hinted, persuaded Henry to withdraw to her palace of Greenwich. Reluctantly the other lords agreed to the withdrawal, paid off their followers, and went home.

Later Henry and Margaret sailed up the Thames to London where the Mayor and Common Council who had received them so joyously only a day or two earlier now begged them to remain and help them fortify the city against any attack by the rebels. Not even the payment of half the King's expenses for the year prevailed however and Henry was over-persuaded by an extremely anxious Margaret that he would be safer in the stronghold of one of his Midland castles. He and she then made hasty preparation and departed for Kenilworth.

Hardly had they taken the road north when they were informed that Bishop Ayscough who had married them in Tichborne Abbey five years before had been dragged from his church and done to death.

'I knew we were right to take you to safety,' Margaret said, emphatically. 'The mayor of London and his commoners are well able to take care of themselves should they be attacked. We are much better advised to lie low in Kenilworth until this wave of madness subsides; while we are there we can send Edmund and Jasper about the countryside sounding out those who are for us and those who are against.'

'Yes, I still do not know why that young Warwick did not support us,' Henry said. 'I do not know where I have gone wrong.'

'You have not erred in any way,' Margaret told him, 'and you must be at peace while we think what must be done to make other people realise it.'

She was quite convinced that she was pursuing a sensible path in removing Henry from danger and she was proved correct when the Kentish rebels entered London and bloody hand-to-hand fighting took place. Eventually the Mayor and the army he had managed to bring together routed Say from the Tower, murdered him and displayed his head upon London Bridge. Those leading members of Henry's government such as the Archbishop Kemp and Waynflete dispensed the king's justice in his absence and Cade and his officers were thrown into the Marshalsea.

'He should have been beheaded,' Margaret cried when she heard this judgement.

'We are told to love one another,' Henry rebuked her gently.

'An eye for an eye,' she retorted, 'in a situation fraught with danger as this is.'

But Cade ran true to his calling and broke out from prison, freeing all the other inmates, and was finally recaptured and mortally wounded while on the run in Kent. His head joined Say's to rot upon the bridge.

Yet, even this show of strength by the authorities did not put an end to the smaller insurrections which broke out like a virulent rash all through the remainder of the summer. Duke Edmund Beaufort's return from France with a defeated and discontented army did nothing to alleviate the situation.

Then, as if drawn by a magnet of opportunity, the Duke of York came home, unasked, from Ireland.

The court was at Woodstock when this news was brought to them. Margaret was sitting in her privy garden with Beaufort, who had been quick to pledge his loyalty to his sovereign, and the two Tudor boys who had been visiting their father Owen in his Welsh home. 'Now,' she said, with the confidence gained from a peaceful and successful progress through the western counties and Beaufort's reassuring presence, 'we shall see if your belief that York had a hand in the Kentish rebellions was correct, Jasper. We must discover if our proud Plantagenet has designs upon our throne.'

'Your grace,' Edmund Tudor cried, glancing at Beaufort, 'there is surely no thought of that! In all the troubles there have been during these past months I have heard nothing but loyalty to our royal brother.'

'You have to forgive him,' Jasper grinned, to the company in general, 'for living in cloud-cuckoo land for since the suggestion that he should marry the little lady Margaret Beaufort has been mooted to him by our royal brother he can think of nothing else.'

'Don't be ridiculous,' Edmund answered with a self-deprecatory smile, 'the child is but nine years old.'

'But enchanting — and a wealthy heiress; yet I'll have you not forget that even if she did have a vision that she must marry you and chose you out of a band of suitors I, *also*, am her guardian and will have a say in her affairs.'

'I know this is important,' Margaret put in a trifle impatiently, 'but we are discussing the Duke of York and I think we should be laying plans to keep abreast of any schemes he has in mind. What do you think, my lord of Beaufort?'

10

Richard, Duke of York, was almost forty in this year of 1450 and without question the most powerful magnate in England. He owned estates which stretched through East Anglia to the Midlands, with much land in the north and important strongholds on the borders of Wales.

He was descended from Edward III through both his father and his mother. His father, the traitorous Earl of Cambridge, had been the son of Edmund of Langley, Duke of York and fourth son of the great Edward; he was, therefore, of less consequence than Henry VI whose grandfather, John of Gaunt, had been the third. It was Jasper Tudor who had first mentioned the ominous fact that Richard of York had a mother who was directly descended from Lionel, the second son. Could it be that Richard might put forward this claim to the heirless throne rather than through that of his father who had been put to death for treason before Agincourt?

Like all Plantagenets Richard of York was handsome, autocratic and popular with the people of the realm. He had also rather more than their usual share of personal pride and lived in high style surrounded by thousands of followers.

His quarrel with the house of Beaufort had begun when John, first Duke of Somerset and father of the little Margaret Beaufort, had sought a commission to lead an army into France almost ten years earlier and had insisted that he should not be subordinate to York. Not only had this wish been granted but money had been poured into the preparations for Somerset's army. York had watched with a jealous and angry eye this preferential treatment and had not been particularly mollified by Somerset's complete failure in the field and his subsequent death which many claimed had been at his own hand.

Drawing on his own monies to pay his troops left to him in France York had fallen out with Adam Moleyns who had advised the withdrawal of York's commission which had then been entrusted to Somerset's brother, Edmund. This had been the crowning insult to York and he had only reluctantly taken up his appointment in Ireland, recognising it as the banishment it undoubtedly was.

It was from there that he now landed at Beaumaris, brushing aside contemptuously half-hearted attempts to prevent him, and marched towards London collecting retainers from his estates on the Marches as he did so.

Henry, much less concerned than those about him, received him in audience. Margaret had tried in vain to stir her husband to resist his over-proud cousin but Henry had, for once, ignored her. She stood now at his side in the council chamber of the Palace and watched York approach the dais. She could almost feel Somerset's resentment as he hovered a half-pace behind her, gripping the pommel of his sword.

As York knelt to the throne the noise which had accompanied him into the chamber died down. His face as he took Henry's hand to kiss it was expressionless and the king smiled upon him benignly. Margaret knew a moment of helpless fury that Henry should be so misguided as to trust a man who could only be seeking self-interest in this unexpected return from Ireland. York wasted no time in presenting his case to the king.

'Your highness,' he said, in that deep and attractive voice Margaret remembered well, 'I am come here into your presence to clear my name which has been grossly dishonoured during my absence in your counties of Ireland. So much so indeed that I was almost prevented from reaching you and putting my case.' Henry made ineffectual and deprecatory movements of his slim white hands. 'My lord, it is my wish,' York continued, 'that you should call before you any man who may show me to have meant dishonour towards you and if he can prove his case I am willing to stand trial as the poorest subject in your realm. What have I done, I ask myself, that your officers should seek to apprehend me and my loyal servants and attempt to throw us into prison?'

'Nothing cousin, you may be assured,' Henry replied. 'Let there be no more of this. If you think you have a grievance write it down and send your complaint through the Chancellor. Come with me and we shall sit down to meat together and you may tell me how Ireland fares.'

Margaret and Beaufort exchanged hopeless glances. This was not the way to deal with York.

By nightfall every tavern in the City of London seethed with the news that the mighty Duke of York had shown the king and that haughty Frenchwoman that he meant to restore to England all those things which for so long had been denied to her. Not since Agincourt had there been such a popular hero. The fact that four thousand of his strongly armed troops dominated all other followers might have had something to do with this state of affairs but it was not everything; Englishmen were tired of the state of anarchy which existed and they blamed a weak king for failing to control his avaricious barons. Now that York had come he would put an end to injustices.

Margaret, while Henry received York's pledge of loyalty and drafted suitable replies, spent her time in prayer that she might conceive and this arrogant man be put down from exalted assumptions.

She was to be in great need of comfort and spiritual guidance in the next few weeks for York succeeded, not only in convincing Henry that he was completely trustworthy but that Beaufort and most of the king's other counsellors were guilty of gross mismanagement and self-interest. Margaret was bitterly reminded of the witch hunt which had ended with the hounding to death of the faithful Suffolk.

York won over the king and then set about bringing the magnates on to his side. Norfolk and the Earl of Oxford pledged him their support. When Parliament met in November London was in a high state of excitement. Margaret, waiting in her apartments in the Palace, heard shouting and the occasional clash of steel as the unruly mob jostled and pushed to watch their favourites arriving in Westminster Hall.

'I am afraid,' she said to Beaufort's wife, Eleanor.

Eleanor, who was experiencing the same emotion, was so amazed to hear the queen confess her weakness that she was shocked into trying to help her. 'Come, I have brought pen and paper, write to your father and I'll set about finding a trustworthy messenger to go to Angers.'

'My father is growing old and thinks more of good food and wine than politics,' Margaret replied in a voice dulled with lack of sleep.

'Well then, your mother or an old friend.'

Pierre? Margaret thought. What does Pierre think of me now after all this time? What was I to him other than a pretty young girl who faced an unknown future? She turned the enamelled ring on her finger and wondered what life might have been if she had not been committed to patching up a botched peace between France and England. What would it be like, she wondered, to be happy? To wander free under soft blue skies, hearing a man whisper words of love and later, perhaps, lie with him in the sweet scented grasses while he caressed her and shut out everything but his delight in her. Happiness is not for me, she told herself; I am one of those born to suffer. Aloud she said: 'Eleanor, why do I not conceive as other women do?'

Beaufort's wife eyed her strangely; the queen was certainly showing facets of her character that she had not suspected. 'Your grace,' she said kindly, 'have you not thought that perhaps it is — it is the king who is at fault?'

'Many times,' Margaret said flatly, 'but could that not be because I do not please him?'

'My lady, that is quite out of the question!' Eleanor was genuinely astounded. 'You are young and attractive — I have often heard you praised.'

'Have you so?' Margaret asked, surprised in her turn. 'I imagined when I was younger that I had the power to make men like me but of late I have felt drained, with no vitality.'

'You are imagining it, and I have heard also, that worry can prevent the conception of a child. Come, write your letters while I send for a page to build a good fire and bring us heated wine. Truth to tell it is so cold and damp today that I am full of the dolours myself.'

Both Eleanor and Margaret were to suffer more before Christmastide for York so succeeded in winning over the Commons that he brought charges against Beaufort which resulted in his being committed to the Tower.

Margaret railed against Henry for his turn-coat loyalty and deliberately went out of her way to be rude to York whenever they were forced to meet. She did, however, prevail upon Henry to see the ignominy which had been brought upon their friend Edmund Beaufort and he promised her that he would set in motion the machinery that would effect his release.

Before this could be brought about Henry rode through the city in the company of York and his other lords making a brave show in well-polished armour. The common people, thanking God that this meant law and order were to be restored in their land, cheered until the houses, crowded together over the narrow streets, echoed like the steep walls of a mountain chasm. Margaret declined an invitation to join her husband and remained at home filling in the hours with needlework. She was, at this moment, in need of a complete new wardrobe but so strained were the finances of the royal household that she had to be content with turning her old dresses and cutting out badly worn pieces. She sighed for the carefree days in Anjou when her mother would conjure silks and damasks from some grateful merchant eager to win his overlord's favours. Henry, it appeared, had no such clients and she was so unpopular that the people would have denied her the homespun and kersey which they themselves wore.

Henry saw that Edmund Beaufort was released soon after the most subdued Christmas Margaret had so far spent in England. She was certain that other people had used their influence to make sure that the king saw the injustice of Beaufort's imprisonment but it was she who was instrumental in gaining her new favourite honours and he was soon made Controller of the royal household. Not long after this appointment was announced Beaufort sought an audience with her.

It was a cold January night when a page escorted him to Margaret's chamber and some suppressed excitement in his manner made her dismiss her waiting women and bid him sit in front of the glowing fire.

'I think we have you to thank for the timber which has recently been delivered to the Palace,' she began hurriedly to counteract a most unwarranted nervousness. 'We were cold over most of Christmas when I understand we were unable to pay even those woodsmen who usually supply the household.'

'That has been seen to, your grace, and I hope most sincerely that you will not be cold again. You must not hesitate to ask me for anything that I may be able to supply.'

Margaret suddenly felt shy of this handsome and fashionably dressed man who sat across the hearth from her and hastily turned the conversation to speak of the new Parliament which had been recalled after the Christmas recess.

'The Commons repeat their request that I, Alice of Suffolk and my friend William Booth should be banished from court,' Beaufort told her.

'But why is this? What have you ever done that they wish to be rid of you?'

'Do you really need to ask that question? I am hated because I lost so much of France in what they can only think of as a wanton and bungling fashion; Booth they hate because he is my friend and Alice they detest because she is Suffolk's widow and all this revival of his sins in this session of Parliament has made them desirous of more blood in revenge.'

'But you cannot think that William really intended to take the throne by marrying his son to your niece, the lady Margaret Beaufort?' Margaret asked incredulously.

Edmund Beaufort hesitated before he replied. 'I would not rule out the possibility that he saw Margaret as the eventual heir to a Lancastrian throne and was so used to wielding power that he hoped to set his son beside her as consort — '

'I cannot and will not believe it!' Margaret cried, rushing to the defence of her dead champion. 'William was ambitious I'll own but his needs were mainly for worldly goods and if I remember rightly the match proposed between John, his son, and the little Margaret was quickly forgotten when an heiress with more money came into his ken.'

'You are probably right, my dear lady,' Beaufort said smoothly, 'but I did not come to speak of the lamented Suffolk but of more personal matters — '

'You approve of the marriage between your niece and the king's half-brother?'

'Yes, I do,' Beaufort replied, somewhat testily, 'my niece is a well-brought-up young woman and Edmund Tudor is a worthy son of his lusty and colourful sire; let us hope that if they marry they are granted a long and happy wedded life. Now, my lady, will you turn your thoughts from others and think for a moment of yourself?'

Margaret looked up swiftly from pouring wine for them both. 'Myself?' she asked while she felt a warm flush sweep up to her throat to colour her cheeks.

'Yes, you, my lady; if I am not mistaken the most lovely and ill-served queen that ever shared the throne of England.'

'My lord,' Margaret said sharply, 'you forget that I am the loyal and devoted wife of a saintly man whose only concern is for the peace and security of his realm.'

'I do not forget that for a moment nor cease to marvel at his good fortune in finding such a consort. I am not thinking of the king — or the queen for that matter — but of Margaret, princess of Anjou and the woman that lies beneath the surface of the devoted wife.'

'How can you dare to speak of such things to me?' Margaret asked with more stunned amazement than anger for his temerity.

'I can easily enough, your grace, when I have but to look into your face to see how you suffer.'

Margaret was caught off guard sufficiently to ask: 'Does it show so much?'

Beaufort chose to ignore her lapse. 'I flatter myself in thinking that I know you well enough to recognise well-controlled misery when I see it. Forgive my presumption in speaking to you thus but it grieves me to see you without the support of a fitting husband and forced, indeed, to lead and encourage the king.'

'I was aware of what I was doing when I consented to become the wife of England's king.'

'Then you were told that our monarch was a gentle soul who should have been a monk?' Edmund Beaufort regarded her levelly and Margaret found herself forced to evade his eyes and look down at the silver cup she held. She discovered that the wine and the warm fire were blurring the edge of the anger she had known at Beaufort's impertinence and it was pleasant, after all, to speak intimately with a man who so patently enjoyed her company. She looked up at him, giving him look for look. 'I was certainly told that Henry had the nature of a saint, but I did not realise that he was — '

'Less than a man in many ways?'

'Perhaps,' she parried.

Beaufort rose from the opposite side of the hearth and poured more wine for them both; he returned, unhurriedly, to his chair, leaning back on its leather support while he stretched his shapely legs to the blaze. Margaret, watching the flames, pictured his lean face, full mouth and bold eyes and found herself smiling.

'That's much better,' her companion said gaily. 'Now I see a little of that fair princess who came to us that winter day so long ago.'

167

'When I believed that the world was a fairy-tale place and all the people of England would love me as the Angevins loved my father. Tell me, Edmund, why it is that the affection the English showed me has turned so obviously to hatred? What have I done that I am so very unpopular? I realise that I am young and have had much to learn but I was prepared to take these people to my heart like my own children.'

'You will make a marvellous mother, my lady.'

For a moment the simple statement hung in the air until Margaret laughed without humour and said quietly: 'Should I be given the opportunity, my lord.' Then, refilling their goblets from the silver ewer, she asked him to tell her of his experience when his lodgings at the Black Friars had been broken into prior to his sojourn in the Tower and he had narrowly escaped losing his life.

Beaufort made light of his sufferings but Margaret had heard from others of the danger he had run and she thought the more of him for his apparent unconcern. Although she pressed him to describe in detail the attack and who the intruders might have been he refused to be drawn and soon

168

turned the conversation to speak of herself again.

'My lady,' he asked, 'which, if any, of your residences is your favourite?'

'Truth to tell I do not know,' Margaret replied, mystified as to the trend of his questioning. 'But if I were to search my mind I should say that probably Pleshy, in the heart of Essex, gives me the most pleasure and seclusion. It is so pleasantly situated that it is possible to forget the affairs of state within its walls.'

'Then may I be so bold as to suggest that you think of the castle as your home and set about furnishing it as you would like to do.'

'There is no hope of that!'

'Why?'

'You know well enough that we have not sufficient money to repair existing fabrics let alone purchase new.'

'Now that I am honoured with the keeping of the household accounts I think you may rest assured that you will be able to indulge your pleasures a little more than in the past. Buy what you want and I shall see that the accounts are paid.'

So her forlorn spirits were revived by that most feminine of all pursuits, the refurbishing of a home, and she did not discover for months that Beaufort paid for the costly damasks and brocades out of his own pocket; and when she did discover the truth of the matter she was past caring about what had become trifling concerns.

11

During the whole of the following year Margaret leaned more and more heavily upon Edmund Beaufort. His spirit for preserving Henry's throne matched her own and upon his insistence she saw to the preparation of armed men. Neither of them (nor their friends at court) blinded themselves to the necessity for such action because before Parliament had been dissolved in the May of 1451 a member of the Commons had plainly stated that York should be proclaimed heir to the throne. The member's imprisonment for his impropriety did nothing to allay the real fears of the Lancastrian party. York meant to have his cousin's throne on his death and if he could not obtain it by fair means he would fight for it.

He put his intentions to the test in January 1452 when he collected together ten thousand men and marched on London. While the Mayor and Common Council failed to admit him and great barons like Salisbury and the magnificent young Warwick watched he withdrew into Kent to stir up those quick-silver rebels of the past.

Henry's army with Beaufort and Margaret as its leaders quickly occupied London and marched on Blackheath where the contenders were brought face to face by those who saw nothing but disaster for England if civil war should break out. Telling York and Henry that it was enough to be carrying on a most unsuccessful war with the French without bringing chaos to their own peaceful land Salisbury and the Bishops of Ely and Winchester persuaded them to make public denial of their differences in a reconciliation service in St. Paul's.

Here Margaret and Beaufort had the satisfaction of seeing their enemy brought to his knees and hear him swear faithful allegiance to his sovereign.

'Now he'll learn who is master in this realm!' Beaufort exclaimed exultantly to the queen as they sat together at a private supper party in the newly furnished solar of her castle at Pleshy a short time after this event.

'Do not let us be too sure,' Margaret said, hastily crossing herself. 'We have the baronage with us at this moment but should it ever come to pass that York wins over young Warwick or the Nevilles I should not like to consider the consequences.'

'There is no fear of that,' Edmund

reassured her, 'they are tied to the throne by blood.'

'But Norfolk hates us — '

'Shall we forget it, now,' Beaufort said gently, 'I have invited a new troupe of dancers for your entertainment and I should not like to think their talents were wasted.'

Entertainments and the obvious admiration of Beaufort did indeed help Margaret to bear the mounting tension at home and the hopeless situation prevailing in France. When the invincible old warrior Talbot wrote from that country to say that without funds the entire territory belonging to England would be lost levies of fifteenths and provisions for putting more than twenty thousand men in the field were granted by Parliament but some funds were withheld from the French campaign as Beaufort warned that the realm had more to fear than the loss of lands overseas, however attractive or lucrative; there was the wolf within the fold.

Most of the year Margaret, with Henry, Edmund Tudor and his young brother Jasper, toured the country stirring up support for the king. In most places Margaret's renewed vitality captured the imagination of the gentry and many people were drawn to their support.

By Christmas a great deal of effort had

been spent on these progresses. Due to the depletion of the royal coffers the festivities were much curtailed, although the satisfactory outcome of the royal visiting and the very welcome news that the English army in France had won back part of the recently lost territories was a better tonic than lavish banquets or expensive gifts.

After the celebrations, in a happier frame of mind than she had known for some time, Margaret set out for Essex with Henry and his young half-brothers. Henry and the Tudors were to go on pilgrimage to Our Lady of Walsingham but Margaret had begged to be allowed to stay quietly in Pleshy awaiting their return.

She came to the pleasant castle on a bright, cold morning soon after Twelfth Night escorted by a strong band of archers and a few of her favourite retainers, among them Isabel Grey who had replaced Eleanor as her chief lady-in-waiting.

Beaufort had sent her a beautiful new mare as an Epiphany present and she looked forward eagerly to trying her out in some hunting through the wooded fields about the castle. As she contemplated a week of peace and freedom Margaret anticipated staying in bed late and meeting people whom she had been forced to abandon during the crisis that

York had brought upon her. Among them was Andrew Doket who was continually sending her plans and schemes for their college in Cambridge; she wondered how she was going to break the news that she would be unable to help him a great deal for the present. There was hardly money enough to feed themselves and their depleted court let alone fulfil grandiose schemes for furthering the schooling of those who aspired to it.

She hunted with great delight during the first and second day of her stay at Pleshy and on the evening of her last outing gave orders for a bath to be prepared for her in her bedroom-cum-solar.

'One of the villagers brought you a couple of ducks, your grace,' Rose told her as she helped her unlace her heavy woollen hunting dress, 'and I have asked the cook to roast them for you and hunt about in the cellars for a cask of your favourite claret. You'll be hungry after a day in this sharp air, I told him, and there is nothing like wholesome food to bring colour into the pale cheeks.'

'Surely I do not look as wan as all that,' Margaret said, smiling, 'I feel better than I have done for an age.'

'Come to look at you properly you look better too,' Rose told her. 'Shall I stay with you or do you want to soak in the water?'

'Just let me enjoy the luxury of being unhurried; the bath smells good enough to wallow in for hours. Where did you find the essences? I thought I had long since finished those I brought with me from Anjou.'

'They must have been some flagons you had forgotten from a previous visit,' Rose said, 'for I came across them in your tiring room pushed to the back of that corner cupboard.'

'Oh, well, I'll enjoy the luxury and try to remember to take them with me when we leave. I must be getting forgetful with so many cares on my shoulders.'

'That would be no small wonder,' Rose sniffed, and went out with Margaret's discarded clothing draped over her arm.

Left alone Margaret lay in the sweetly perfumed water relishing the pleasure of the peace and the soothing warmth. The fresh air had made her drowsy and she thought of nothing but her own enjoyment. Only because she began to feel the cooling of the bath did she reluctantly rise from the wooden tub and wrap herself in the linen towel which the thoughtful Rose had hung beside the fire.

When she was dry Margaret put on a loose chamber gown and took a brush to her hair. Rose knocked softly upon the solar door and came in with four other girls who removed the tub and set a table beside the hearth. Rose bustled about plumping cushions and rearranging the eating implements until she finally led away her underlings. 'Will you have the Lady Isabel to supper with you or would you prefer to remain alone?' she asked as she was about to close the door behind her.

Margaret yawned. 'I'm so sleepy that I think I had better not attempt to be sociable; just bring me my food and I shall go straight to bed.'

When Rose had gone she picked up a book which had come in a parcel from her father and mother at Christmastide and turned the title pages slowly. Her eyes seemed too heavy for reading and the light from the reduced number of candles which she had ordered, too dim to permit her to concentrate on the handsome illuminations so she closed the covers and sat back. In what seemed only a few minutes she was startled by a tapping on her door and she made an effort to sit up and receive the Master Butler and his servants who would be bringing in her supper. In her sleepy state it took her a moment or two to realise that it was Rose once more and that the girl was bubbling with suppressed excitement.

'Your grace, you have a visitor. I have tried to tell him, in vain, that you are enjoying a few days' rest and quiet but he insists that he must see you.'

'Must see me?' Margaret queried. 'Who is it that thinks he has the right to intrude upon my privacy?'

'My lord the Duke of Somerset,' Rose said, hardly able to hide the glint in her eye.

'Beaufort?' Margaret said, unbelieving and still half-comatose, 'but I thought he had gone to his estates. Bring him to me, Rose.'

As soon as the girl had gone Margaret forced herself fully awake, her sense of well-being disappearing in her immediate anxiety that some ill had befallen Henry. She was reproaching herself for allowing her husband to go to Norfolk without her when Edmund Beaufort was announced and strode into her room to fall on his knee and take her hand in his. He brought the fresh cold of the January night with him and she saw, in a flash, that he brought her no illtidings; his mouth on her hand was not the perfunctory salute of a courtier for his queen. Somewhat unsteadily Margaret told Rose that her guest would sup with her and would need a chamber for the night.

'I thought, my lord, that you were at Bletsoe spending Epiphany with your sister-in-law and the little Lady Margaret.'

'I did spend a couple of days with them but

I felt that I had been absent from you for almost a month and that I might be needed.'

'And you think you were right?'

Beaufort did not reply at once but looked down upon her from the hearth where he stood until she was compelled to look up at him. 'Yes, but since I find you, unexpectedly, alone I am not so certain that the need which I had imagined is the same which I now discover.'

Margaret's pulses began to beat more quickly but she was saved from immediate response by the arrival of attendants with supper.

The cook had excelled himself with the ducks and had made a sauce equal to any Margaret had tasted in her father's home. The wine which had been discovered from the cellar was also excellent as was the sweeter one which accompanied a rich apple pie served with a basin of thickly whipped cream. Margaret's mood of pleasant well-being returned and, as the servants removed the table and the dishes, she gave orders that she was not to be disturbed and that Rose and Beaufort's squire would be summoned when they were needed.

'Need we sit so formally on these damnably uncomfortable chairs?' Edmund asked her. 'Won't you allow me to put cushions here for us in front of the fire?'

He took her hand and she stood up, the loose chamber robe falling open to reveal her bosom. With a half-muttered exclamation Beaufort took her in his arms and kissed her. Still in the dream-like state in which she had been since her languorous bath she swayed against him until she heard herself say: 'Take me to bed.'

When she awoke in the chilly darkness of the winter night her first thought was not of the gentle Henry but of Pierre; by allowing Edmund to make love to her she had betrayed that deep and personal passion which she had for so long harboured. But she could not cry for what she had done and, awoken now to the realisation of what a true union of man and woman could mean, she put out her hand to touch Edmund and give herself to him afresh. She realised with a small shock of disappointment that she was alone and chided herself for her foolishness that she could have imagined that he would have dared to remain with her. What was the price he would be made to pay if he were discovered in the act of adultery with the king's wife? Margaret shuddered and calling on every particle of the iron self-control which she had taught herself over the years compelled herself to sleep.

Edmund departed on the following afternoon after a morning spent in attempting to work on state papers. She was grateful to him for making no assumption that she would want him to remain.

When the king came he brought not only his half-brothers but Cardinal Kemp and after greeting Margaret with his usual gentle courtesy and affection called together all those ministers who had travelled with him to discuss the next Parliament which was to meet in Reading in March. Margaret forced herself to pay proper attention to what might be one of the most important meetings of recent times; there were, after all, signs that some of the outbreaks of violence between lords and their followers were being contained and that a return to dominance in France was only awaiting more supplies and troops. Yet, as she listened to the wordy debates and the plans to mollify the Commons, she could not help thinking of the night she had lain in Beaufort's arms and there had been nothing in the world but the giving and receiving of physical pleasure. She had little experience upon which to call to know whether or not the Duke of Somerset was an accomplished lover but he had stirred her senses and left her with the most delicious of memories. She was sensible enough to realise that this instance of shared passion was not the instigation of a love affair but the outcome of circumstance. And, if that circumstance should provide England with a long-awaited heir, so much the better. Nothing could serve to put York out of countenance more than to present the people with a lusty man-child. While she tried to listen to the ways and means by which Talbot and Shrewsbury might be reinforced with extra men-at-arms she was already savouring the discomfiture of the overbold Richard of York when he discovered his declared enemy was great with child.

'I wish that Beaufort were here.' Henry's soft voice broke through her thoughts and she found herself blushing. This would not do to behave like a guilty maid-servant and she straightened her spine and said, in a voice that she hoped was not too loud: 'My lord of Somerset was here but three days ago on his way to Norwich to hear cases in an Oyer and Terminer and told me that he will return to pay his respects. I am certain that you may expect his coming tonight or tomorrow at the latest.'

'That is good news, indeed,' the elderly Kemp said with relief. 'His handling of the last session of Parliament was nothing short of masterly and we need him now when we plan to keep these unruly Commons from teaching their masters how to rule.'

No other questions were asked about Beaufort's visit and Margaret knew a curious sense of deflation; only later when Jasper was handing the company wine did she find her young brother-in-law eyeing her with a little speculation in his humorous face. Of the two boys he was far more worldly than the intense and high-minded Edmund Tudor and Margaret feared he might probe the subject of Beaufort's visit. However, he rejoined the discussion, leaning back against the wall where he had stationed himself, absent-mindedly fondling the ears of two Irish wolf hounds who were his constant companions while he gave his elders and superiors his complete attention; when he spoke his comments were apt and constructive. It was Henry's intention to mark this Parliament by conferring peerages upon his brothers so that they might take their place among the other lords and Margaret was glad that they would be able, in future, to call upon their real support. Life, it seemed, had suddenly taken a more rosy turn.

★ ★ ★

183

Parliament met in the refectory of the Abbey of Reading on the sixth of March. It was notable for its tranquil atmosphere and the creation of Edmund Tudor to the earldom of Richmond and Jasper to the earldom of Pembroke. The young Tudors were both formally declared legitimate and large estates and grants were conferred upon them. Margaret had put a brave face on it when Henry had asked her to relinquish Pembroke to Jasper for she was reluctant to give up any source of revenue; but in the general euphoria accompanying this Parliament any concession seemed easier to bear.

Margaret had, at the time, her own secret and great source of satisfaction for she knew, without doubt, that she was going to have a child. Throughout the first week of her stay in Reading she had no opportunity of speaking alone with Edmund Beaufort but one evening, when Henry was at his meditations, she took a cloak and went to walk in the Abbot's privy garden.

This walled and pleasant place was secure against the biting east wind which had accompanied the royal party to Reading and there seemed to be a hint of spring in the softly falling dusk. Beaufort saw her as he looked down from the window of the room in which he was lodged and hastened down to be with her.

'My lady,' he queried, 'I find you well?'

'Very, I thank you; and who would not be with so successful a Parliament? Are you not happy that we are able to disperse and meet again in London after Easter?'

'I am, of course, and can hardly believe that all went so well that even the contentious Nevilles were civil.' They had come now to the furthest corner of the garden where a small summer-house had been set in the angle of the wall. 'You will not find it too cold to sit with me here for a moment or two?'

'I could not be chilled for that which I carry within my womb sends a glow through me which touches my very heart.'

'Margaret!' Beaufort put his arms about her as if in protection. 'Is it mine, the child you carry?'

'I do not know, my lord, in truth.'

'The king? He comes to your bed?'

'Now and then,' she replied simply, 'but I do not believe that he is capable of siring a child.'

'Then your son and mine will rule England, my dear.' Edmund said, fiercely exultant.

'Perhaps,' she replied, mildly, 'for we cannot count upon its being a boy.'

'You are content?' he asked, putting her

185

hand against his cheek.

'I am more happy than I had known possible. If you have any idea of what it means to be an unloved, alien and barren queen you will realise that my life has changed completely. I do not care,' Margaret said, echoing the strength of his own exultation, 'what happens now for I know that I am as other women are and have not failed in that duty which was most expected of me.'

'You do not mind that the child might be mine?'

'Not only do I not mind but I am glad that there is a possibility that you, who have been so loyal a friend, might share in my happiness.' Of her own will she leant forward and kissed Edmund upon the mouth. 'But do not think that this means that I am to begin a sordid affair that might endanger you, me or the precious burden which I carry; I shall, for ever, think affectionately and gratefully of you and I pray that we may work together to preserve my husband's throne.'

'You know that you can count upon that. York hates me and I would rather die than see him dominate England.'

'Do not speak of dying — it is bad luck.'

'Then tell me if you intend to speak yet of your pregnancy?'

'There is time enough to make public the

186

good news; let us savour it in private for a while yet.'

'As you will and I hope that you will let me ease the burden of your financial worries. I know that the royal coffers stand in debt to the sum of some three hundred thousand pounds and I cannot bear to see so brave a woman suffer.'

'You are more than kind.'

'May merchants wait upon you tomorrow with cloths and some staple foodstuffs?'

'They will be most welcome. We had best go in, my lord, for there are those in the court who have sharp eyes when they search for other's sins.' Once more she kissed him. 'Thank you, Edmund.' It was the first time she had called him by his name since they had lain between the coverlets of her bed in Pleshy and his arms tightened about her. She pushed him away gently. 'Do not make things more difficult for us both,' she pleaded and resolutely walked towards the Abbey.

Here, almost as if she paid the price for the short interlude of people she found a messenger awaiting her from Angers with the unwelcome tidings that her mother had died a few days before. So sudden was the news that she burst into a rare flood of public tears and hurried away to her own apartments on the arm of a sympathetic Isabel Grey. How

187

she had wanted to tell the brave Isabella that she was to bear a child and now she was gone without hearing the good tidings. Recovering herself she called for pens and paper and resolutely began to write condolences to René; if she were sad he would be devastated for they had been married since he was thirteen and she ten and suffered together worse privations than even their daughter knew.

The Parliament which was resumed in London was as successful as that which had taken place in Reading with grants for the army in France and peace prevailing between all Henry's nobles. He dismissed them until November, telling them to enjoy their summer hunting, and left London to make another of his extended progresses through his realm.

Margaret and he made their way to a hunting lodge in the New Forest at Clarendon. Here Margaret intended to tell her husband of the coming child; she had delayed for reasons which she could not define clearly but had felt in need of time to prepare herself.

On the first day after their arrival they followed the scent of a wild boar and came home triumphantly with a royal-sized beast. Henry was flushed with the exercise and the success of their expedition. While Margaret dressed to sup with him in his solar she planned how she would tell him of the coming child.

She was braiding her hair to coif it under a netted headdress which had been a present from Edmund Beaufort on her last birthday when Henry's squire rushed into her rooms imploring her to come to her husband. Puzzled by the young man's obvious distress Margaret put down her hairbrush and went with him immediately.

She was never to forget the sight which met her eyes for Henry lay as if half-dead on the bed in his chamber. She rushed to his side and knelt beside him.

'Henry,' she cried, 'what ails you?'

He turned his head with the greatest difficulty, trying to focus on her face. 'It is nothing,' he managed with difficulty. 'Better in the morning.'

Frantically she looked up into the faces of those about her. 'Fetch me towels and hot and cold water,' she ordered.

Margaret sat by him until darkness fell when his physicians begged her to take some rest.

Kemp, hastily summoned from Winchester, led her from the bedside.

'I am frightened,' she said, 'for I have

always had it in my mind that his mother might have handed on the dread madness of her father Charles of France. But, if I am right, the King of France only suffered attacks when he had heard bad news and just now all seems to be going well for his grace — unless he has heard something which has caused him grief?' Had he perhaps learnt that she was expecting a child and that it might not be his? It was a risk which she always ran. On this score her mind was soon put at rest for Kemp hesitated and then led her to sit on a backless chair.

'My lady queen, his grace did indeed have grave news on his return from hunting for an embassy was awaiting him to tell him that both Talbot and the Earl of Shrewsbury have been killed in France and our cause is lost, perhaps for ever. I cannot begin to tell you — '

'Then do not,' Margaret interrupted him peremptorily. 'We cannot waste our energies on needless grief at this moment, for we have a sovereign sick unto death and we shall need every ounce of our strength to help him recover. We have enemies, my lord Bishop, nearer than Guienne!'

12

By the middle of August Henry, King of
England, had lapsed into a state of madness
in which he lost control of not only his mind
but his body also. He could neither walk, sit
up nor stand and it was pathetic to see him
lie upon his bed staring vacantly into space
oblivious of those who hovered always at his
side to minister to him.

Margaret was the most faithful of his
nurses, tending him with her own hands night
and day.

'We must see that at all costs no word of
this illness comes to the ear of Richard of
York,' she said to Archbishop Kemp and
Edmund Beaufort one evening in August
soon after Henry lapsed into complete
unawareness. 'Nothing would give the man
greater satisfaction than to know that we are
tending a hopeless invalid.'

'Surely not hopeless,' Edmund said, gently,
'for if we are to compare him with his
unfortunate grandfather, Charles of France
would recover from his attacks and take up
the reins of government.'

'I spoke hastily,' Margaret said; 'with this

heat and as I am at the moment I tend not to think very clearly.'

'That is not to be wondered upon,' Edmund comforted her and turning to the old bishop he asked him if he would be kind enough to say vespers so that the queen might be left in peace. Kemp fell upon his knees as quickly as an aching back would allow and made short work of the evening office; he was, to tell the truth, tired with long watching at the king's bedside and was grateful of an opportunity to depart early to bed. When he had finished his prayers and psalms Beaufort helped him to his feet and politely led him to the door telling him that he would soon follow him.

'Boy,' he called to a page who stood at a respectful distance, 'bring cyder from the still room and see it is well chilled.' He returned to where Margaret had taken up her position on a seat at an opened window. 'May I read to you for a little while? My wife brought a new copy of 'The Book of the Duchess' from Alice de la Pole's while she was staying at Ewelme and she thought you might like to hear it?'

'I should, very much,' Margaret said while she wondered if Eleanor would be so anxious to please her if she knew the truth of the relationship existing between herself and

Eleanor's husband.

Beaufort read for a time until Margaret quietly thanked him and took the book from his hands. 'I shall never be able to express my gratitude for all that you have done to help Henry and give me courage during this terrible time.'

'I wish, my dear, that I had been permitted to be more to you than just an ally; you will never know how many times I have wanted to take you in my arms and show you that I care for you more deeply — '

'Don't speak of it,' Margaret said quickly, 'for I have already been punished for my sin.'

'Then you are exonerated,' Edmund said with a wry smile. He did not pursue the subject for he recognised that his queen was sorely tried by the ordeal of nursing Henry and carrying the child. 'But I am not the only one who has stood by you, your grace; you have stalwart supporters in Kemp, Roos and the Tudor boys; not to mention the Northumberlands and the Nevilles.'

'When they are not fighting among themselves,' Margaret replied with a small laugh to mark the lessening of tension as their personal situation was temporarily forgotten. 'They are a hot-headed lot at the best of times and with the present lawlessness in the air they are given more scope than usual to quarrel.' She dropped her bantering tone and asked Beaufort earnestly if he considered that they had managed to keep secret the nature of Henry's illness.

'I think we have done quite well; there are bound to be Yorkist spies in your household but you have been so dutiful in your care of his grace that it would be difficult for an outsider to fathom a great deal. What worries me a little is how you will deal with the formalities of spreading the good news once your child is born.'

'Surely it will be sufficient to make an announcement?'

'After eight years of a barren marriage?' Edmund took her hand now and held it whether she would or no. 'You realise, don't you, that the Chancellor and the Archbishop of Canterbury, to name but two, will have to be present at the birth?'

'How barbaric!'

'But very necessary if it is not to be said later that an unknown infant was smuggled into your bedchamber to be hailed as the long-awaited heir.'

'I shall consent to those measures only if the officials remain in an ante-chamber and you are of their number.'

'It shall be done as you desire, and may

God speed the day of your delivery.'

In the early light of the thirteenth of October Margaret was awoken with slight pains in her back. She made no move to arouse Isabel Grey, who slept in a truckle bed in the corner of her room, but bore the increasing sharpness of her labour until Rose came to wake them both with ale and manchet bread. The waiting woman did not need to be told of Margaret's approaching travail and swiftly sent for the attendant midwife and the two physicians who waited upon the king and queen.

Despite her bold approach Margaret had not realised how exhausting and difficult her ordeal might become and although the black-gowned medical men were to say later that she was the best patient they had ever attended she was, nevertheless, entirely drained of energy. She could only smile in exulted triumph when she was told that she was the mother of a fine, lusty son and received the congratulations of Henry's ministers as if through a mist. She did manage to whisper to Kemp as he stooped to bless her and the child cradled against her that Henry must be informed of the birth immediately in the hope that the good news would shock him into recovery. Of Edmund Beaufort she was only vaguely aware as she lay back against the pillows and drifted away into sleep.

★ ★ ★

But Henry was entirely unmoved by the joyful tidings brought to him and even the sight of the child failed to arouse him to anything like his former self.

While Margaret lay gathering her strength notices were sent out summoning the great magnates to attend a Council to mark the birth of an heir. Edmund Beaufort, Duke of Somerset, made it plain that York should not be included in the invitations and managed to override those who felt that bygones should be forgotten and Richard welcomed. Edmund himself was persona non grata with several members of the Council who thought he had acted unwisely in antagonising the youthful Warwick by snatching some of his hereditary lands earlier in the year: Warwick was the most powerful young baron in the country and this was not the moment to be alienating men who had well-trained retainers at their back.

When, indeed, Northumberland, Norfolk, Warwick and the older Salisbury arrived in Westminster to congratulate the queen and discovered that York was excluded from their number, they made it obvious that he should be told; not only told, but sent for immediately.

Beaufort came to Margaret's private apartments and raged, helplessly, against his fellow peers. 'We shall never be able to govern this country in peace while York is of our number; if that man is invited to take part in the Councils I shall most certainly resign.'

'But, my lord,' Margaret protested, 'you have so recently become the little Edward's godfather and promised to protect him; how can you neglect him thus?'

'I said nothing about neglecting him — or you; but I cannot and shall not sit at any conference table with that arrogant, hypocritical York while he decides what shall be done with my son and the realm that will one day be his.'

'Oh, hush for pity's sake,' Margaret pleaded.

'I'm sorry,' Beaufort said contritely, pacing about the room.

'I know how you must feel,' Margaret said, soothingly, 'and I am much recovered now and mean to make my presence felt.'

'I'll not shelter behind a woman's skirts, however handsome,' Beaufort growled. 'I think I'll go home for a week or two and see to my neglected estates. I'll not go, don't fret, until I know definitely if that wily fox intends to come to London. By all the holy saints was there ever such a pretty kettle of fish on the brew! Doesn't that man realise that he makes war between our dissonant nobles inevitable?'

'Surely there is no question of taking sides?' Margaret asked, in the greatest alarm.

'Not at the moment, but our land-hungry magnates only wait the opportunity of getting at the throats of their so-called friends and equals. Without a wholesale war to fight in France there must be some means of enriching themselves.'

★ ★ ★

It was, perhaps, from this moment that Margaret made her decision to prepare herself to take upon her own shoulders the responsibility of her husband's kingdom. She had but to look into the wooden cradle in which her baby son lay to know that she would sacrifice her life in order to keep his inheritance.

She was glad of her newly found courage for Beaufort, true to his word, left the Council on the arrival of the Duke of York; followed, much to Margaret's private dismay, by the venerable and trusted Archbishop Kemp. If she had a friend in whom she could have confided without fear Margaret would have admitted that she was almost pleased to see the departure of the turbulent Edmund Beaufort but heart-sick at the absence of the Archbishop. Edmund had proved himself a true Plantagenet when she had produced a son. If only Henry might revive into some resemblance of his former gentle self!

But this blessing was not forthcoming. York arrived in London on the twenty first of November and began at once to express his undying loyalty to the king and his great desire that peace and prosperity should be paramount in the realm. Although there were those who had reservations, he was kindly enough received and spoke with such sincerity that in no time he was being begged to accept the role of Protector of England and those who slid to cover behind his strength (which was manifest in the enormous number of armed men who had accompanied him to London) began to speak of impeaching Edmund for his conduct of the French war.

Margaret, suckling her son, and still waiting upon the helpless Henry, heard these fateful decisions in the privacy of her apartments at Westminster. She was glad that Edmund had decided to go to his estate and pondered upon the wisdom of sending a trusted messenger (if one were obtainable) to tell him to remain there. While she thought over the matter Beaufort himself was announced one chill December evening while her household was making preparation to spend Christmas at Windsor.

'My lord,' she cried, rising to greet him with outstretched hands. 'You should not have come here!'

'I should like to see the man who would stop me. Let me look at you . . . in truth I think you are fairer than I remember. See, I have brought you and the child gifts for St. Nicholas tide.'

'Edmund,' Margaret said desperately, 'do you not know that York and his henchmen plan to impeach you?'

'I had heard rumours, the ill-begotten son of a hog, but I'm not afraid of him. Where is the child? Take me to him.'

Margaret led him to the crib which stood close to the small fire; the baby stirred and whimpered as Beaufort stroked the side of his down-covered head. For Margaret it was a moment of almost overwhelming sentiment and tears fell down her cheeks unheeded. At last she and Beaufort left the sleeping baby and returned to the parlour where, despite Margaret's pleas that he should be gone, Edmund drank a goblet of wine and settled himself beside the hearth.

'Is that the best you have in firewood?' he demanded. 'I gave instructions that you should be sent regular supplies.'

'We have received none since we returned from Clarendon,' Margaret told him, 'but I have given instructions that wood shall be brought to the Palace from the Enfield Chace. Don't worry now about household matters, but drink up and be gone, for pity's sake.'

'I am no coward to hide myself away; if York intends to take me let him do it here, where I am most at home.'

Almost as if on cue there was a loud and peremptory knocking upon the door of the private apartments and a frightened page scurried into the parlour saying in a choked voice that officers of the Protector were demanding entrance to arrest the Duke of Somerset.

Edmund stood up, leisurely stretching his arms above his head. 'Why do they wait? I am prepared to go with them to the Tower or whither they want; they may take my body but my mind and spirit will remain here, serving the sovereign and his queen.'

'Order the men away!' Margaret cried.

'That is no easy matter with a crew of some twenty, armed to the teeth, standing outside your door,' Edmund replied lightly. 'Fret not, my lady, for I have been imprisoned before and it will not last.'

★ ★ ★

At Windsor Buckingham came to see how his king fared and was so moved by the plight of the luckless Margaret and her infant son that he personally took the baby in his arms and brought him into the room where Henry sat gazing with lack-lustre eyes into an endless nothingness. His impassioned pleas to his sovereign did nothing to rouse him.

'I confess that I am at a loss to know how to advise you,' Buckingham said, taking his velvet bonnet from his head and scratching his bald pate.

'I have resolved to ask Parliament when it meets to appoint me Regent of the realm. Only thus may I protect those I hold most dear.'

'You are a brave woman, my lady, and upon my oath I am bound to say that I'll back you. Will you take the child now and see if his grace is moved by the sight of his heir?'

But there was no flicker of interest in Henry's eyes and eventually Margaret and Buckingham withdrew handing over the little Edward into his nurse's care.

'Have you news of Somerset?' Buckingham asked.

'He writes frequently and is well.'

'He must have bribed half of the watchmen in the Tower then! But Somerset was never a man to lie down under an injustice and I have it on good authority that he has spies everywhere. Has he told you that York's eldest son had been set up in London with his own establishment?'

'Edward of March, your nephew? But he is still a child, is he not?'

'He is a youth I should say, some twelve years old and forward with it.'

'It isn't difficult to see how York's mind is working.'

'Indeed not,' Buckingham shrugged.

★ ★ ★

Margaret's attempts to become Regent of England were studiously ignored when Parliament met again and a sad blow came in March when the stalwart Kemp died. The lords appointed a committee of picked men to journey to Windsor to see for themselves the state of Henry's health. Despite all they could do to rouse the king they failed and Margaret watched them depart for London with a sickening sense of frustration. In a few days she heard that York had been confirmed in his Protectorship which was to last until the little Edward, who had been proclaimed Prince of Wales, came of age.

Margaret had to be content in that for after Buckingham's visit she had been ready to believe that York would press to have his own son Edward of March named as a claimant to the throne.

★ ★ ★

The rest of the year passed in tending Henry and watching her son grow strong and affectionate. Margaret occupied her leisure in writing to her bereaved father, fighting the lost causes of her servants and clerics and spending what little money she was able to obtain from her estates in equipping the army which the imprisoned Edmund told her was vitally essential.

On Christmas day 1454 Henry shook off his illness as if he had been in a deep and refreshing sleep and became aware of those about him. Squires who hurried to Margaret's apartments where she was preparing to hear early Mass begged her to bring the prince and come with all speed.

To her great delight Henry knew her and she had no difficulty in making him understand that the child which she held out to him was her son and the heir to the throne.

Later in the day Henry asked for his advisers and was grieved to learn that his faithful Kemp had died. 'Where is Edmund Beaufort?' he asked when he had crossed himself and closed his eyes in prayer for the deceased archbishop. 'He is not dead I hope?'

When he was told that Beaufort was in the Tower Henry showed more signs of restored vivacity than at any other news he had been brought. 'He must be released immediately. Who sees to the governing of the realm?'

So Edmund was restored to the high positon of trusted counsellor and York writhed as he saw him appointed to the captaincy of Calais in his place. York's chagrin was further heightened with Somerset's friends taking over most of the offices held by Yorkist men. He knew that it was a matter of time before he was excluded from the Council. When this happened he made for Ludlow taking with him his twelve-year-old son, Salisbury and the handsome Warwick.

'They have gone,' Margaret cried exultantly to Henry and Beaufort, one evening in early April. 'Now we can go back to running the country as we did in the olden days.'

'Let us call a great Council to meet in Leicester, towards the end of May, and show the people how we intend to govern in peace and security,' Beaufort said aloud while he added to himself, 'and find out if York went in peace or in order to make preparation for war.'

13

The royal party set out from London on a fine day towards the end of May in high hopes of reconciling the dissenting parties at the great Parliament in Leicester.

Edmund Beaufort, Duke of Somerset, riding at the rear of the cavalcade with his two most loyal followers Thorpe and Joseph had hardly reached the village of Islington beyond Finsbury fields when a lone horseman rode up to the captain of the guard and demanded to speak with Beaufort himself. The captain of the guard disdainfully told the man to take himself off and not try to speak with those so patently his superiors. Edmund heard the altercation and thanking the captain for his courtesy beckoned the man to his side. With a look which was clearly intended to bring instant death to the offender the captain waved him towards Edmund.

'My lord,' the messenger said, taking off his leather hat and bowing slightly, 'I bring you word from the Duke of Northumberland that my lords of York and Neville are on their way to Leicester.'

'Are they indeed?' Beaufort asked sharply. 'With many retainers?'

'It was impossible to judge for a Percy is not over anxious to come too near a Neville, be he armed or not.'

'Thank you all the same,' Edmund said, 'I am glad to know, at least, that York is on the move. Take this for your pains and fall in behind with my company.' The messenger deftly caught the coins flung to him and rode back to take up his position as far distant from the discomfited captain as possible.

Edmund brooded on the significance of the news he had been given but made up his mind not to impart anything to Margaret or the king until he had more idea of York's intentions. At Watford, where they spent the night, he took the precaution of doubling the guard and sending out scouts to the north.

To his dismay the latter brought back the unpleasant tidings that York, Salisbury and Warwick with the other Nevilles had passed Leicester in a formidable march and were approaching Ware.

Beaufort hurried his contingent to St. Albans sending out messengers to round up as many loyal men as possible. He could not now keep the news from Margaret or his fellow peers and as they assembled at an inn to make plans to withstand any military activity by York and his followers, they heard that Richard had taken up arms against them.'

'We must fight them.' Margaret stated flatly. There was an uneasy exchange of glances between the men gathered round her; many of them had no desire for a death struggle with an army which contained relations such as brothers-in-law or cousins.

'Of course we must,' agreed Northumberland, who had now joined up with the King's party. 'We are being given a marvellous opportunity of ridding the country of those pestilent Nevilles.'

'First let us send an emissary to seek out their intentions,' Henry said, so quietly that all listened.

'Of course,' said Clifford, Stafford and Wiltshire almost in a trio.

'Rubbish,' muttered Henry, the young Earl of Dorset, who as Beaufort's heir felt he was of great importance in the matter. His father gave him a withering look and nominated three people to proceed to York's encampment to discover the reason for their march against their king. These messengers did not return for a considerable time and Beaufort was thinking of sending Jasper Tudor, now Earl of Pembroke, to discover the reason for the delay when they appeared at the hastily improvised headquarters of the royal army to say that the Duke of York wished no ill against the majesty of his king but wanted Henry's word that he would pledge the unconditional surrender of Edmund Beaufort into his hands.

'I shall never agree to that,' Henry said, displaying that calm strength which so often came to him in moments of crisis.

'So we shall fight them,' Northumberland said with satisfaction.

'Outnumbered by a thousand men,' Beaufort muttered and despatched Margaret, her son and the other ladies of the party to safety of the ancient abbey. Margaret tried to persuade Henry to accompany her but if he was calm he was also obstinate and he refused to come, saying that his place was with those who fought loyally for him.

The battle was no prolonged affair but was quickly brought to a climax by the unexpected generalship of Richard Neville, Earl of Warwick, who outfaced the royal men and their retainers in less than an hour.

Henry, standing weaponless on the side lines of the skirmish, was slightly wounded in the shoulder and was led away, protesting, to the abbey.

Edmund Beaufort, sword in hand, was everywhere encouraging laggardly fighters but knew all was lost as he saw Northumberland and Clifford fall and watched, helplessly, their retainers sneak away between the houses. He found himself driven back against the inn, where so recently the fateful decision had been made to fight, and stumbled into the darkness of the interior in the vain hope of escaping through a back window. One or two of his men pushed in with him and were quickly followed by shouting men wearing the spanking new livery of Warwick. Beaufort felled the first cursing soldier who rushed at him and fended off two more who crowded in from the street but, seeking to protect himself from his immediate foes, he failed to see a great ox of a man who brandished a giant cleaver which he brought down with his full strength on Beaufort's head.

The death of the second Duke of Somerset saw an end of the fighting and though there were those who said it was necessary to despatch Buckingham who had been wounded York would hear of no more bloodshed.

Margaret, stunned, received the victorious York as she tended Henry's wounds. Fiercely fighting back tears for Edmund's death (which was quickly and callously revealed to her) she put her arm about her husband and defied York. 'My lord,' she said proudly, 'you may have robbed England of her most valiant champions but never forget that I am Henry's most devoted defender and that, while he and my son live, I shall work without ceasing to keep their kingdom for them — and them alone. At this moment we are helpless and friendless, it would appear, but be warned that I am like a tigress when I am roused.'

York bowed with mock servility and gave low orders that the king and his consort with the prince were to be taken back to London in all honour and comfort.

As she was escorted out to a saddled horse, with a nurse carrying the baby prince, Margaret distinctly heard a woman in the gaping crowd which had gathered outside the abbey say to the gossip at her elbow: 'Poor brat, what will become of him now that his father is slain?'

Burning with indignation Margaret drew her veil about her face and allowed herself to be lifted to the horse's back. 'I'll show them what will become of Edward,' she thought savagely, 'for he has me to protect and guide him and I am worth two of any English lord.'

She waited while the strange horse she had been given moved restlessly under her until Henry was led from the church and mounted on a dappled grey. He looked about him until he saw her then, like a storm-bound ship finding a familiar harbour, lightly touched the flanks of his steed with his square-toed boots and moved next to her. 'What has England come to this day that brother fought brother and our devoted Edmund has been killed?'

'Don't fret, but put your faith in God and ask Him to continue to give me strength to act for us all; your cause is mine and I shall never give up while there is breath in my body.'

* * *

So began those vicious battles which later came to be known as the Wars of the Roses; and if York hoped to bring peace to the realm by fighting it out at St. Albans he was to be desperately disappointed.

* * *

The rest of the year was marked by a return to the squabbles of the warring lords in the west country and in the north. York was by no means as popular as he had been in the past and his method of installing his favourites in the high places of office made him life-long enemies.

Margaret spent all her energy in trying to keep Henry well and in good spirits but he was often morose or feverish and at the time of the marriage of the Lady Margaret Beaufort to Edmund Tudor was so indisposed that he was unable to travel to Bletsoe to give the couple his blessing. Margaret sent Jasper to Edmund and his new bride to invite them to begin their married life in the isolation of Jasper's home in Pembroke castle.

'Tell them to go there and breed in peace,' Margaret said, hardly able to keep the weariness from her voice. 'We are in need of strong Lancastrian supporters.'

'But what of the new Duke of Somerset?' Jasper asked.

Margaret eyed him levelly. 'He is not of the same stamp as his father and is rash and too quarrelsome.'

'I see. Yet you have other staunch and loyal men?'

'Of course; there is Buckingham, the new Archbishop of Canterbury and, I hope, you and your brother.'

'You know well enough that we would never desert you or our illustrious brother.'

When Jasper had left her Margaret broke a pact which she had been keeping with herself for the past two years and wrote to Pierre de Brézé. Once started upon the letter she found it was as if she had opened the flood gates of a dam and she covered page after page with her bold and impetuous hand.

When this missive had been entrusted to a secretary, who vowed he would rather die than surrender it into any hands other than Pierre's, Margaret found her mind clear and her spirit revived. What if York had sent away all those faithful to Henry and herself? The wounded Buckingham, whose heir had died of the injuries he had received at St. Albans, was still her friend as were the fiery Ralph Cromwell, Lord Beaumont and the Earl of Devonshire. True enough, at this moment, they were occupied in their favourite pastime of fighting personal battles with their neighbours but that was solely for the reason that York had dispensed with their services and given them time to brood upon slights, imaginary or otherwise.

'I shall go to Tutbury,' she announced decisively to Elizabeth Grey who had replaced her mother-in-law Isabel. 'There I shall be out of the way of this proud lord and shall have peace to plan my campaign.'

'You mean to keep your word?'

'About defending my own? Yes, without question.'

'You will leave the king here?'

'For the moment,' Margaret said, 'but I shall take the prince and bide my time about bringing his grace to be with us.'

'You are a bold woman,' Elizabeth told her,

her eyes rounded in her softly pretty face.

'Would you not protect your baby sons and your husband?'

'Of course.'

'Well, then, is it not more important for a queen to look to her own?'

★ ★ ★

While Margaret set about her plans to restore Henry to her side and spend her time during this summer in her Midland estates to call together her followers a new force was making itself apparent in the Yorkist party. This was in the shape of the highly ambitious and splendid Earl of Warwick; with his handsome good looks, genial and expansive character he had a way of winning the people to him and those who had been present at St. Albans had passed on his commands to attack the lords and leave the commoners alone. He was a popular figure wherever he went with his red-coated soldiers carrying on high his banner of the ragged staff. He had persuaded York to give him the command of Calais in the place of the dead Edmund Beaufort and while he awaited the outcome the wrangle about the perpetual backlog of unpaid wages he spent his time, when not at Warwick castle with his wife and two daughters, endearing himself to the ship chandlers and shipwrights of the Kentish ports. He hardly forgot a name and was always ready to share a flagon of wine or down a quart of ale. In the shadow of a weak and hapless king he became the figurehead of the people and crowds flocked to see him as they never did for York.

It was York himself who kept his young cousin from going to Calais when at last the differences about pay had been settled for he needed his strong support to counter Margaret's success in rousing her turbulent party.

For Margaret was able to call a Council to Coventry in the September of that year and York and Warwick coming boldly to confront her found themselves humiliated and forced to beg forgiveness from Henry, whom Margaret had once again nursed to comparative health. Seething with fury at having been so entrapped York returned to his estates to plot his next move and Warwick set sail at last for Calais.

For weeks afterwards men talked of nothing but the strange portents which had marked his eventual crossing of the Channel. Men crossed themselves and awaited what the omens presaged.

In the January of the following year

Margaret received a monk from France who had come straight to her from Pierre. He brought her a letter which made her forget the rigours of a bitingly cold day with little fuel and scanty food.

'My lady,' she read, 'my greetings and loving affection. Your noble uncle of France was distressed to hear of the plight in which you found yourself at St. Albans and sends you his warm sympathy. I, on the other hand, was struck with horror that you should have been treated in such a disgraceful manner and you may rest assured that I am seeking every means to aid you — '

Margaret read and reread the contents of this, the most welcome letter she had ever received, until at last with much regret she threw it upon the fire and stirred the logs until the blaze had consumed every trace. This was not a document to treasure.

Hardly had Margaret resumed her chair and taken up a roll of accounts from the Household chest than Jasper Tudor was announced. He was frozen with the cold and his lean, attractive face showed signs of deep fatigue.

'My lady, I come to beg you for leave of absence to go to my estate in Pembroke — '

'Why, Jasper, what takes you there? Your sister-in-law has not miscarried with the child she is bearing?'

'No, the lady Margaret is well but my brother is dead of the plague in Carmarthen.'

'How terrible!' Margaret cried. 'You must leave at once; we cannot have the Lancastrian heiress in open danger. How sad about your brother; he was so well and full of life when last we saw him. How came he to fall ill of the plague?'

'It would appear that he was riding about the countryside in the matter of keeping the king's peace when he took part in a small skirmish. One of his men was grievously wounded and died in his arms: Edmund spent the following night in the priory of the Greyfriars at Carmarthen where he was taken ill with the plague; the lady Margaret rode from Pembroke to nurse him _____'

'In her condition?'

'Apparently so, but he worsened and died almost as she reached his side. Poor young lady, I cannot bear that she is left alone at so sad a time. Will you permit me to go to her?'

'Of course,' Margaret said, putting as much warmth as she might into her voice for she was conscious of the fact that with Edmund dead and Jasper away from her side her own party was considerably weakened.

'I shall come back any moment that you send me word,' Jasper assured her, as if he read her mind.

'Go in peace.' Then with more warmth in her tone asked: 'When is the child expected?'

'At any moment.'

'Then be gone.'

The king was saddened at the sudden death of his own half-brother. 'We had a true Lancastrian there,' he told Margaret, 'within whose veins ran blood that could not be swayed to other factions.'

Margaret Beaufort gave birth to a son on the day following Jasper's arrival at Pembroke. He was a lusty child and was named Henry after the king. His birth helped his royal namesake as he grieved for Edmund's wasted young life.

With the spring Margaret and Henry started upon a royal progress, meeting and talking with as many people as possible as they moved through Staffordshire, Cheshire and Herefordshire. Margaret was generally pleased with the reception which they were given by townsfolk and burgesses alike and discovered that the sight of the baby prince, now growing into a sturdy and handsome child, promoted good feelings wherever they went.

She and Henry were leading their retinue towards London when news was brought to them that the French fleet were making for

Calais. The sweet May sunshine seemed suddenly mocking as the darkest thoughts clouded Margaret's mind; was this Pierre's attempt to help her? Having no one with whom she might discuss her innermost doubts she spent the evening of their sojourn in Berkhamstead castle on her knees in the chapel. In her happiness that Henry's people seemed to have forgiven her for her French ancestry she had almost forgotten the underlying intention of Pierre's message to her; remembering only, when she called it to mind, the subtle expressions of love he had conveyed.

Please God, she prayed, let the French fleet be bent on piracy and nothing more.

But Pierre was bent on burning out of Calais the glorious Warwick, who was beginning to make himself a nuisance as he became friends with Philip of Burgundy and the exiled dauphin Louis. Charles of France, who was Pierre's master, had ordered harassment of this troublesome nobleman from England and Pierre seized his opportunity to serve both his king and the woman who had appealed so desperately for his help.

When he discovered that the wily Warwick had built up a miniature fleet about Calais he turned towards the English coast and came ashore to ravage Sandwich, the main source of supply to Warwick's garrison. Leaving a burning town behind him he went blissfully back to France loaded with booty.

Margaret wept when she received the news and could not stifle her sympathy for the London merchants when a little later a convoy of their goods was looted from Portuguese merchantmen by the same French fleet.

Warwick was sent money to replace his stores by the Court of Common Council from the City of London and became their hero when he engaged the Spaniards and saved a similar convoy bound for the Thames.

Warwick sailed back to London on a triumphant wave of popularity to answer the King's call for a meeting of the Council. His appearance with several hundred of his troops attired in his flaunting livery did nothing to appease the young Lancastrian lords who were out to avenge the blood of their slain fathers.

'Keep the peace, my lord,' Margaret pleaded with Buckingham, 'while we are in London we are not among friends. If we have to fight these belligerent lords let it be in the north where we may call upon support and the King of Scotland stands at our back.'

'I'll do my best, my lady, but I have it on good authority that Warwick sees himself as the coming power in England.'

'Does he so?' Margaret asked coldly, her eyes narrowing and her voice taking on the harsh edge which seemed to have superseded the husky quality which had been one of her chief attractions. 'The young popinjay (he was almost of an age with herself but she chose always to speak of him as a childish upstart) had better think again before he sets himself up as a puppet-master.'

But the peace was kept and York and the queen walked behind Henry, Salisbury and Warwick to a reconciliation ceremony in St. Paul's where promises of friendship were made with great sincerity and ease.

And in no time at all were as sincerely and as easily recanted and broken.

14

Margaret, with Henry with the five-year-old Edward Prince of Wales, returned to Cheshire where she immediately set in motion the processes of amassing an army. She pawned or sold every large piece of silver and plate that she could find and kept spies about the country for news of any movement of troops against her own.

When the Yorkists, under Warwick's father, Salisbury, scored a minor victory at Blore Heath she countered with a blow near Ludlow which sent York, Salisbury and Warwick scuttling for the protection of Ireland and Calais.

It was too much to hope that they would remain within these sanctuaries and Margaret did not cease in her efforts to strengthen her army and her cause. She made overtures to James II of Scotland, promising him many of the northern counties of England if he would assist her with men or armaments and bribed her English loyalists with promises of land and titles.

True to her expectations Warwick returned to England, magnetising troops to his banners and captivating London with his charm and authority. While Warwick marched north Buckingham summoned the king's army and taking Henry with them set out for Northampton where they dug themselves in on a moated site close to the River Nene.

Henry, attended by two squires, sat disconsolate in pouring rain while Warwick sent emissaries to request an audience.

'Tell him he does not deserve an audience!' Buckingham shouted. 'What means the Earl of Warwick coming with so large a force against his grace? Tell him he shall not come to the king's presence, and if he does he shall die.'

The fight was on and this time the Yorkists had a new and gallant champion in the seventeen-year-old son of the Duke of York, Edward, Earl of March. Standing six feet four this golden-haired giant fought hand-to-hand with Lancastrians pushing them back across the muddy banks they had built to protect themselves until their ranks broke in confusion and bloated bodies floated down the Nene. For six hours the two sides fought one another and at the end a weary and befuddled Henry was escorted to London by a triumphant Warwick. Buckingham, Shrewsbury and many other lords lay dead in the squelching mud while the bodies of Henry's squires stared lifeless into the grey heavens.

Warwick, vowing loyalty to the king, set about the business of forming a government while the heartbroken Margaret fled with her son to the safety of Jasper's castle at Harlech. He, tearing himself away from the guardianship of his beautiful widowed sister-in-law at Pembroke, sent messengers throughout his domains rallying the Welsh to the aid of his imprisoned half-brother and his impoverished queen.

Margaret's fortunes were at their lowest ebb and she spent hours of each day sitting with Jasper while she racked her brain for possible sources of wealth and aid. She had now only a couple of attendants and no jewels or daily plate for she and the young prince had been waylaid on the journey to Wales and robbed of what meagre possessions she had brought away from Coventry with her.

'Do you not think, lady, that it would be best to make your peace with Warwick?' Jasper suggested one morning when the hills beyond the castle precincts were ablaze with heather and his mind kept reverting, whether he would or not, to the girl he had had to leave in his stronghold at Pembroke.

'Never!'

'But he continually asserts that he has

Henry's wellbeing at heart.'

'He had no one's wellbeing at heart but his own; he wants power and he means to have it.'

'Very well, we can do nothing but force the issue against him. Now, Lady Margaret, will you not ride with me for an hour or so? The day is so splendid and I hear that fallow deer are to be had with ease in the hills.'

Margaret reluctantly agreed to go out with him but insisted that they took Edward with them. Jasper promised to fetch the child while Margaret went to her apartments for her cloak. He found Edward on the battlements with an old grizzled sentry who was watching his antics with benevolent amusement. Edward was brandishing a miniature sword and swearing lustily. As they descended the stone staircase to the bailey Jasper asked him what he was doing.

'I was chopping off the heads of the Duke of York and Earl of Warwick,' his nephew replied with relish.

For a moment Jasper thought of his other nephew at Pembroke and his heart misgave him. What was the queen about that she allowed her son such warlike pursuits? Was it she who instilled hatred or was it inborn? Not for the first time he wished that he might go back with all haste to Pembroke and watch

Edmund's widow tend her son and his little bastard daughter Helen with gentle hands and soft and doe-like eyes. He was in love with her, he knew only too well, and was faced with the devastating problem of finding another husband for her because his absence on the king's business left her unprotected. Who could he trust in this all important task?

The hunting was successful and the fresh air whipped colour into Margaret's pale cheeks and gave her an appetite for the good food which Jasper provided. When supper was cleared away Rose offered to play chequers with her and she accepted the offer gratefully. Jasper had taken himself off on some secret business of his own and she was craving for company.

Margaret was barely awake on the following morning when Jasper asked if she would receive him. She arose, hastily pulling on a woollen shift and a borrowed chamber-robe of furred velvet, for it was chilly in the sparsely furnished castle and a far cry from the warm serenity of her father's dwellings upon the Loire.

In the anteroom of her apartments she found Jasper awaiting her with the Duke of Exeter.

'My lord of Exeter,' she cried, hurrying to meet him with both hands held out. 'This is most welcome and unexpected.'

'I have come as quickly as possible, your grace, to pledge you my renewed support and that of the men whom I have collected together. I bring you, also, tidings of great importance.'

A servant entered carrying a tray on which were brown bread and foaming tankards of ale. While he set these upon a table Jasper, Margaret and the duke sat down; immediately the man had departed the queen rounded on Exeter. 'Tell me your news.'

'York is in London.'

'Indeed? For what purpose? To worm his way into Henry's confidence?'

'Hardly that; he has done with the play acting of honouring the king for he claimed the throne for himself.'

'What think you of that?' Jasper asked Margaret.

'I think it is high time we rid the realm of this troublesome upstart. But was his presumption well received?'

'Not at all and much to his discomfort he had to climb down from the high pedestal on which he had endeavoured to set himself — '

'Ah, we have more faithful friends than I thought!' Margaret said with satisfaction.

'We must not be too confident of that,' Exeter said, slowly. 'We have few friends in

London at the moment. It was York's own people who would not allow this travesty, strangely enough, for whatever their quarrel with — you, my lady,' he said after a slight hesitation, 'all are loyal to the king.'

'I know,' Margaret agreed, her voice heavy with disillusion, 'they are such fools but they can still see what will befall if they deprive the kingdom of the Lord's anointed ruler. What was the outcome of the matter, my lord of Exeter?'

'That the Duke of York prevailed upon your husband to nominate him as heir to the throne,' Exeter told her bluntly.

'I cannot believe it,' Margaret cried. 'Jasper, is this true?'

'Regretfully, it is; I can only think that my brother was forced into such a decision.'

'Then we must fight them!'

'Yes,' Exeter agreed, 'there seems no other way. But I have not told you all the news and I hesitate to pile woe upon woe.'

'Out with it,' Margaret commanded him sharply, 'nothing you have to tell me could hurt as much as that which you have already broken to me.'

'Your husband's cousin — and Jasper's also — King James II of Scotland has been killed by one of his own cannons while laying seige to Roxburgh castle — '

'How terrible,' Margaret said and impatiently brushed her eyes with the back of her hand to stop her tears. 'This Roxburgh, is it in England?'

'Yes, it is.'

'Then I have another death at my door for he was coming south in an attack upon our mutual enemies. What have I done, my lords, that blood lies like snail's shine upon any path I tread?'

'Take heart, lady, for doubtless James of Scotland welcomed any opportunity to plunder the rich castles of the English,' Exeter said in an effort to comfort the pale, distraught woman who sat toying with a piece of bread before him.

'Exeter brings some good tidings,' Jasper put in, 'for the queen mother of Scotland sends you her greetings and bids you come to her side; she has told Northumberland that she will make every effort to provide you with troops.'

'But that is marvellous!' There was no disguising the queen's elation at this, but her joy was arrested almost as once. 'But with what shall I pay them?'

'Exeter and I have money for you which you can repay when the times are happier; both of us have sent messengers to all your old supporters bidding them finish their personal quarrels with their neighbours and come to us with arms and men.'

'That is most good of you. Now that I am determined to put an end to York's claims I shall leave nothing undone to gain support for Henry. Can you spare me a reliable man to go to France to the court of my uncle?'

'Of course,' Jasper answered quietly; handing her paper and quills he and Exeter took their leave.

'What do you make of her?' Exeter asked him as they gained the privacy of Jasper's own rooms.

'A brave and frustrated woman but I cannot help thinking that she is misguided in her policies. I know we must do all we can to help her — but I think that if she were to be less partisan she would find the English nobles better friends than enemies.'

'You are right. I am sure that she is hated in England; I have seen the most scurrilous notices about her pinned to the doors of churches and town halls and the like. The crudest of these do not hesitate to call the Prince of Wales a bastard and credit the queen with every type of infamy. Have you any views about — ' Exeter hesitated, recalling that Jasper was the half-brother of the king.

'You mean do I think that Henry might

have been cuckolded?' he asked steadily. 'Well, anything is possible is it not? Now, if you will come with me I'll go down to the harbour and see if a reliable captain can be found who is willing to risk his neck in carrying the queen and her son to Scotland.'

★   ★   ★

Soon after Christmas York, heady with the success of being nominated the heir-apparent hurried north to deal with a Lancastrian army which was plundering his estates. He did not wait for Warwick or his own charming and gallant son Edward to join him but, supported only by the aging Salisbury and his second son, skirmished with some troops near Worksop and rushed headlong into a pitched battle outside Wakefield.

Here, lacking the generalship of Warwick and the giant-like strength of Edward of March he and his son Edmund were hacked to pieces in an overwhelming Lancastrian victory. Salisbury was taken prisoner and later put to death. Two days later the Lancastrians came into York and stuck the gruesome heads of York and Salisbury on pikes above the walls. A wag with more wit than compassion stuck paper crowns on their bloodied hair to serve as a reminder to other

233

overweening upstarts.

Margaret heard the news of the victory with gladness for now Scotland and her uncle in France would be more willing to give her aid. The young and widowed queen mother of Scotland showed her willingness to help by signing a mutual treaty of alliance in which she pledged her help in return for the surrender of Berwick by the English. Margaret was only too pleased to give up this bleak and meaningless fortification to her friend in Scotland, having no conception of the age-long struggle which had existed between the two kingdoms for its possession.

She was elated by the kindly reception she had received in Scotland both from the shy, nine-year-old king and his mother and was further encouraged to grasp the omens of success by letters which came to her from Pierre in France. He told her that Charles was giving him permission to aid the new young Duke of Somerset who had a beach-head in northern France and to put a fleet to sea to contain Warwick's.

Margaret and Exeter with a motley collection of Highlanders and Lowlanders left the Queen Regent of Scotland at Lincluden and marched south. In the north of England she met up with Northumberland, Clifford and Somerset, newly arrived from France.

She could hardly credit her eyes when she saw that each supporter brought with him armies that could be numbered in their thousands.

'We shall win,' she told Exeter as they mounted their horses on a windless, bitter day in January 1461, 'for never has a righteous cause had such a magnificent army.'

In truth she could look with pride upon the countless men who, if they did not all sport the same livery, at least wore the ostrich feather badge of her son the Prince of Wales.

All down the Great North Road her army was swelled by more men. 'You shall never live to regret this day!' she harangued them with pride. 'We go south to liberate the most gentle and kindly king that has ever sat upon the throne and you shall share in our joy and our victory.'

When she was told that her Scottish troops were plundering houses and even churches as they accompanied her she was inclined to dismiss the stories as jealous tales fabricated by Englishmen who could never miss an opportunity of speaking ill of their hereditary foes. But in Stamford, where she knelt in prayer in one of the many beautiful churches which graced the town, she lifted her head from her devotions in time to see two bare-kneed Scots creeping down from the high altar bearing a magnificent branched candlestick in their grimy hands. Startled and never less than brave she sprang up and remonstrated with them, so shaming them that they dropped their spoil and fled from the church.

After this she gave orders that stricter watch was to be kept in order to stamp out plunder and rape. She was saddened to realise that her officers had little or no control over their Scottish allies.

On February seventeenth at St Albans Margaret's army overcame a force led by Warwick which included Arundel, Norfolk and Suffolk. In jubilation she was reunited with her husband after a separation of over six months. Henry cried with delight at their meeting and knighted the Prince of Wales. 'For you have been a gallant champion in bringing your mother safely to my rescue,' he told the flushed and proud child.

In peace and thanksgiving the royal family retired to rest in the hospice of the Abbey. Exeter came almost at once to the queen. 'Your grace, this is not the time to sit idle and at ease; we must press on into London. Do not give Warwick time to rouse the citizens.'

'My lord, the Yorkists are utterly routed, what can they do now?'

'They can reform and attack us once more.'

'We cannot march now; not with this army against London. Would you have these lawless barbarians tear apart the city churches and bring down for ever the wrath of the Londoners against us? Take heart, Exeter, for I have had news this day that my good friend de Brézé is commanded by my uncle to render us any aid we may require.'

'If we march now we shall need no aid but our own,' Exeter said, with desperation in his voice.

'We shall wait for Jasper Tudor,' Margaret said, grasping at any straw to prevent her moving with her undisciplined army against the capital of her country.

It was not for some days that she was to learn that Jasper had been defeated in a battle at Mortimer's Cross and put to flight. When she heard she most reluctantly gave orders for the king's army to move. But it was too late. Warwick had worked his magic upon the citizens of London and had charmed them into rejecting Henry as their king and accepting the dazzling Edward, once Earl of March, as their monarch.

No force could contain the vigour and enthusiasm of these two cousins as they stampeded out of London and turned the queen's victory at St. Albans into flight.

Margaret's army, shouldering its plunder, melted away and only with the greatest difficulty were her captains able to hold ten thousand of the multitudes who had originally set out from the north in her train.

At Ferrybridge, near the village of Towton, the hounded Lancastrian army turned and faced its pursuers.

Thousands perished before the victors of St. Albans broke and fled for their lives.

Margaret, heart-weary and deeply grieved for those who had fought for her, waited within the safety of York until Somerset and Exeter, miraculously alive after hours of the most bitter fighting, rushed into the hospice where she sheltered with Henry and her son and urged them to flee with all speed on whatever mount they could find.

As darkness fell the fugitives once more took the road north to sanctuary in Scotland.

15

'I shall never give in, never.'

'But what use is it, my dear, if Edward is now king and the people do not want me?' Henry pleaded.

'It is not a question of what the commons want,' Margaret replied coldly. 'You are their anointed sovereign, blessed with the Holy Oil that sets you above other beings; and apart from that the throne belongs to our child.'

'If you would pray more, Margaret, your soul would be at peace.'

'I can never be at peace while I stagnate here and Edward decides our future for us. He has gone from strength to strength — why, even death has helped him by taking Uncle Charles of France and putting that cold cousin Louis on the French throne. I hate him for imprisoning Pierre de Brézé; if he had been free I should not be languishing here now.'

'We have sent messengers to France, what more can we do? All Louis seems to do is imprison them.'

'He is a calculating man who has plotted for years from the safety of the Burgundian court what he would do when he became King of France and he is now practising the art of playing Edward off against us and vice versa. Oh, I think I shall go mad if we have to remain at the Scottish court for another winter. Margaret of Gueldres tries to hide the fact that we are not as welcome as we were but it is like two women sharing a kitchen to have two queens under the same roof. Why don't you send more messengers to Louis?'

'To what end, my love, to have them thrown into prison like Somerset and the rest?'

'Oh, Henry, you are too kind and too reasonable, come and walk with me a little in the privy garden; at least the spring is coming and hope must stir somewhere for us.'

And it did seem as if fortune showed them a glimpse of possible kindness only two days later when Henry, Duke of Somerset was admitted to her chambers in the castle of Edinburgh. She stared at him at first, unable to believe that any of her friends had been able to break out from Louis' prison and come alive through the constant guard of the proud new Yorkist King of England. 'My lord, is it really you?'

'It is, your grace, and I am delighted to find you and our sovereign lord safe and well.' The young man, a pale counterpart of his aristocratic father, knelt to Henry in unfeigned homage. Henry remonstrated with him mildly and waved him to sit on the only other chair in the scantily furnished room.

'Is there wine, my dear?' he asked Margaret.

'There is enough, certainly, for the most welcome visitor we have had for months.'

'For my part I am so happy that you have been given sanctuary by the Queen of Scotland and that you have been, if I may be permitted to speak my mind, heedful of all that Hungerford and I wrote in our letters.'

'It has been well nigh impossible to remain here with nothing to do while Edward of York branded us with acts of attainder and put to death all our faithful lords and servants. During last year I feared to receive a letter because they brought me nothing but the names of people executed who had been kindly disposed towards me and my family since I had first stepped on to English soil. Your mother, is she well?'

'She keeps very quietly to her estates and goes no more to court but her health is as good as one might expect. Have you news, my lady, of Pembroke or Dacre or Clifford?'

'Jasper Tudor was in Ireland when last he sent me messengers but I know that he crosses into Wales from time to time.'

'He is a brave man with a sentence of death hanging over him.'

'And are not you, my lord?' Margaret asked quietly. 'Tell me, when you were released were you able to seek an audience with King Louis?'

'Yes, and I was treated most royally with gifts of gold and silver; it was bewildering to be dragged from confinement and shown such courtesy.'

'Then you think the King of France looks more kindly upon our cause than that of Edward of York?' Margaret asked, eagerly grasping at this straw of encouragement.

'I should say that his grace of France is a most canny diplomat and having very little cause to favour York's party and their Burgundian connection he leans towards you, in your distress. He is, madam, your cousin and they say that blood calls to blood.'

'It did not when Louis was fighting his father during the early part of Charles' reign,' Margaret said with a laugh, 'but he may have changed after all this time. My lord, you bring me news of the most comforting nature. I think the moment has come for me to go to Louis in person and plead for help. Will you come with me?'

'Go to Louis?' Henry asked in distress.

'Yes, my dear, he can refuse to aid me

242

when ambassadors crave assistance in our name but he cannot, face to face, repel my supplication.'

She was a different person now from the listless woman who had risen to greet Somerset and the young duke saw in her what his father must have admired. Weary as he was with the difficult and dangerous journey he had undertaken to come to Henry and his queen he was filled with admiration for her bravery and heard himself agreeing to set out as soon as possible.

'Hungerford hopes to join us here in a day or two. We came separately to arouse as little suspicion as possible but he will bring a small band of men with him which will be useful in guarding his grace, the little prince and yourself.'

'I shall not bring my lord husband or my son with me; that is not to be thought of.'

Somerset turned to look at his dethroned king and found Henry was reading a missal, apparently no longer interested in what was going on about him.

'Very well, madam, and with your permission I shall set about finding suitable ships and trusty sailors.'

So in April Margaret sailed from Kirkcudbright with Somerset and a small retinue. She had parted from Henry and the Prince of

Wales in tears but once aboard the small vessel which had been fitted out with some modest comfort for her, Rose and two waiting women she set her mind and heart on meeting her father and beseeching Louis to grant her money and troops to overthrow the usurper who now sat upon her husband's throne.

Mercifully, the weather in the Irish sea was fairly calm and the convoy came into Ecluse in Brittany with Margaret in good health and steadily rising spirits. Confined as she had been for months with Henry and her small son as her only companions apart from servants, she now enjoyed the society of other men and women. Somerset, she discovered, was as determined in his hatred of the Yorkists as she was. Unlike the pious Henry who was prepared to take ill fortune as a punishment for earthly failings and suffered in gentle melancholy, Somerset thirsted for revenge and a return to power. He was a tonic to the frustrated Margaret.

In Brittany she was kindly received by the duke and given every assistance for her journey to Rouen where Louis, she heard, was then staying.

Outside the city her cavalcade was met by a band of Rouen's most distinguished citizens in their best robes who greeted her with effusive addresses and presents. As they were completing perhaps the tenth of a series of long orations a cloud of dust to the east heralded the approach of another body of horsemen.

'Louis' troops by look of the standard,' Somerset murmured to her when their horses backed together for a brief moment.

'Thank God,' Margaret grimaced.

The gentlemen that now came to a halt with a flurry that disturbed the dignity of the pompous townsmen were indeed part of the king's suite. Margaret waited with growing impatience to hear their invitation to join their sovereign in Rouen.

She could hardly stifle her chagrin when the last burgess bowed to her and handed her an illuminated scroll and the first of the knights suavely welcomed her in the name of the King of France. 'Monseigneur regrets that he has had to depart for Chinon, but trusts that his fair cousin of England is well and that the lodgings which he has had prepared for her in Rouen will be pleasing.'

Margaret knew better than to ask why Louis had left so precipitately and with all the grace she could muster thanked them for their courtesy and followed them into Rouen.

Later when she and Somerset and her ladies were eating a hearty meal in the hall of the 'Golden Lion' she allowed her temper to vent its spleen upon the devious Louis. 'I shall go straight to my father in Angers and put my trust in him that he can aid me so that I have no need to apply to the King of France. Does he think that I am some unknown princess that I must crawl to him on my knees?'

So, on the following morning, in brilliant May sunshine she and her retinue made for Anjou; she was returning home after seventeen years and she could not help thinking of the time when she had set out for England in the flower of her youthful beauty to marry an illustrious king. How differently had fate treated her from what she had expected.

As they rode up the short hill to the castle at Angers she was wearing her only good gown, a pale green silk which she had purchased in Rouen. Sempstresses had worked throughout the night to complete it so that she might greet her widowed father with some degree of pride. René was awaiting her within the shadows of the gateway and he hurried forward to lift her from her horse and embrace her; she was blinded by tears at the comfort of his arms and clung to him like a child. When he held her away from him and looked into her face she saw that her father had grown stout and elderly but his eyes still twinkled as she remembered them and his voice was warm with affection.

'Come in, my love, and meet all your old friends.' He threw the reins of her mare to a groom and led her across the courtyard to his apartments; together they climbed the staircase and hand in hand came into René's parlour.

Unlike the austere English castles with their narrow windows which permitted little daylight the room was flooded with sunshine and for a moment Margaret was blinded. She heard her father say: 'Dearest Margaret, you remember Pierre of course.' Someone took her hand and raised it to his mouth.

'I thought you were in prison,' she stammered, groping for words to express her tumultous joy at this reunion, so unexpected and so miraculous.

'I was, but Louis saw fit to release me when I told him that you were coming home and I wished to be of service to you.'

She dared not look at him in case she betrayed those emotions which she had restrained so successfully during the terrible years since they last met but the sound of his voice was like balm and the touch of his hand a caress. Other people came to greet her and René guided her about the room, her arm drawn through his, until it was time to sit at the loaded boards which had been prepared for her homecoming.

It was not until musicians played for the company that she found Pierre at her side once more.

'I do not know where to begin in all that I have to ask you, but may I tell you that I have prayed for you every day and watched your valiant struggle with the deepest admiration?'

'I did what any woman would have done for a weak and gentle husband — and I intend to carry on the fight if only I can persuade my father to give me funds.'

'You have no hope of that,' Pierre told her simply, while her delight in his company was temporarily dimmed.

'Why?'

'He is beggared by the continuous fighting we have been engaged upon with Burgundy and he has had no opportunity of replenishing his treasure chests.'

'He never did have any money, so I suppose I was hoping for a miracle. There will be nothing for me to do but approach Louis, whether I wish it or not.'

'He will not refuse you — no man could. You are welcome to my fortune, such as it is: I owe it to you in retribution for allowing you to make so disastrous a marriage. Will you ride with me tomorrow so that we may speak together in private?'

She looked at him, changed from the courtly gallant who had attended her betrothal in Tours, but perhaps more comforting and dependable in the assurance of early middleage. His hair was luxuriant and greying where it lay against his cheek bones but his body was as lithe as the young squires who lolled against the tapestries.

'Yes, if it can be arranged.'

* * *

Pierre, who was nothing if not determined, saw to it that it was arranged. When he awaited Margaret, soon after the household had heard an early Mass, he was alone except for a handful of men-at-arms. 'I had something of a task in persuading your father that I was quite able to take care of you,' he chuckled, 'but when Jeanne told him that she needed his help in arranging the mummers for the banquet they are giving in your honour this evening he seemed quite content to remain at home.'

'This second marriage of my father's, is it a happy one?' Margaret asked as he helped her to the ornate saddle of a very much better mare than that on which she had ridden into

Angers on the previous day.

'Nobody could have rivalled your mother in his affections, for it is a long time from twelve to forty-seven to be married to one woman, but although Jeanne is so much younger than he they seem to be very fond of one another.'

'I'm glad, for I should hate to think of him as lonely.'

Pierre said nothing but patted her hand and, then leaping to his horse, they cantered off down the steep cobbled street towards the road for Les Ponts-de-Ce.

It was an exhilarating morning but already the sun was hot and Margaret recognised the day as one of those that would be ideal for an alfresco meal beneath some shady tree. She did not say anything to Pierre of her thoughts for she had no idea if he intended to prolong their time together or return her to Angers in an hour or two.

While they spoke in a companionable way from time to time she contented herself with looking at the familiar and well-loved landscape of her home. She saw that the young vines were in good leaf and that the gardens of the little cottages were already filled with vegetables and soft fruit. The air was sweet with the scent of wild flowers and birds sang above their heads.

Margaret filled her lungs and luxuriated in the warmth. Scotland, that bleak and distant country, seemed another life and her wan husband some character in a play. Even Edward, that precious son for whom she risked so much, faded into the background of her mind. Was the country of her adoption so unattractive that today seemed so beautiful? Or was it that in England she was so beset with the cares of government that she had no time to appreciate its beauty?

At the meeting place of the rivers Maine and Loire Pierre signalled his small retinue to keep their distance and, dismounting, he helped Margaret to the ground.

'Shall we walk a little on the bank?'

They walked for half a mile past a few scattered houses until they came to the edge of the village; here was an inn with a courtyard covered with a trellised vine. The host and a servant in de Brézé livery greeted them; while the innkeeper led Margaret to a table already set with pewter plates and goblets Pierre spoke with his man who loped off into the surrounding trees.

'Now,' he said, joining Margaret at the table, 'you can begin to tell me all that has befallen since we met last.'

He poured wine for her and she drank thirstily, savouring the flower-like bouquet. 'I

251

cannot start my tale of woe until I have thanked you for everything that you have done to help me. You cannot know what it has meant to me to think that you supported me however trying was my ordeal.'

'And it has been an ordeal?'

'Yes.'

'Tell me about Henry first.'

So she began, haltingly at the beginning but with gathering momentum, to unburden herself of the tragedy of her marriage and the warring factions of England. Pierre listened attentively, pouring more wine and serving her with pâté and freshly baked bread when the host brought them.

At last she sat back, her voice tired with the effort of making her case clear to this man who mattered so much to her.

'This Warwick,' Pierre said, wiping his mouth with a napkin, 'seems to be the power behind the Yorkist throne. We have heard much of him in France; what is he really like?'

'A man of great charm but one that I have hated since I first set eyes upon him. He is ambitious and filled with an overbearing pride. I have always thought, as he has royal blood in him through his Beaufort connections, that his real aim is the monarchy for himself.'

'But England would never stomach that?' Pierre cried, incredulous. 'By the saints, France would be filled with would-be kings if all those who had regal blood in their veins sought to be crowned.'

'From what I hear Louis is making sure that he rules France alone and lets no one forget that he is the highest prince in the land.'

'He is a strange man indeed, quite different from his father — '

'Whom you served with such loyalty? Has Louis really forgiven you for that?'

'I hope so; but we are speaking of your life, not mine at this moment. Tell me of Henry; do you love him?'

'What is love?' she parried.

'Ah, there is a question which has worried the world since before the time of Plato; what is it indeed?'

'If you mean, does my heart ache for his helplessness, then yes I do. He is pathetic, but gentle and kindly and would have made a perfect monk. Had he been able to live at peace in a cloister he would never be attacked by these devastating periods of madness. It seems cruel that he has had to suffer so much. How do you think it comes about that a man like Henry V should have such a son?'

'He takes after his mother, it is as simple as that; Katherine de Valois handed on to him the legacy of her father's madness.'

'But her other children, the Tudors, show no signs of any ailment; Jasper is a man of strength and considerable character. He has been of much comfort to me.'

'Now tell me of your own son — does he inherit his father's weakness?'

Margaret picked up her goblet and looked away from him to the broad Loire where the trees on the opposite bank were mirrored like a tapestry in the tranquil waters. 'He is a true Plantagenet,' she answered slowly.

'You mean he is not Henry's child?'

'No,' she whispered and began to cry. They were the heartbroken tears of a woman who had guarded a secret for more than ten years, cradling it in guilt. It was too late to assess if he would hate her for the admission and she bowed her head on to her arms in an abandonment of weeping.

'Poor Margaret,' Pierre said, 'but you only tell me what I had already suspected.'

'You do not think ill of me?'

'How could I? England had to have an heir. Come, dry your tears and eat some of this splendid strawberry tart which the innkeeper's wife has made especially for us. Let us talk now about how I am going to help you in the future.'

'You are so kind,' Margaret said, shaking her head in amazement, 'I do not know what I have done to deserve it.'

'You are the niece of my late-lamented king,' Pierre answered with a smile. 'But I hasten to inform you that is the least reason why I want to assist your cause; nor is this the moment for speaking of what truly makes me your servant.'

'May I ask you one thing?' Margaret took a knife and cut two wedges of the tart. Pierre helped them both to mounds of thick yellow cream.

'You may ask me anything you will.'

Margaret hesitated and put a spoonful of the strawberries into her mouth; when she had eaten it she asked in an almost incoherent rush: 'Your wife, she is well?'

'She is, and has plenty to occupy her at the Chateau de Brézé with our son married so recently — '

'Married, your son? Is it possible?'

'More than possible,' Pierre replied, drily. 'Like your father I was married young. But that was not the question you intended asking me, was it?'

Margaret shook her head.

'You have answered it, all the same. I think we should be returning to Angers, and on the

255

way you can instruct me how I should best
deal with Louis. Will you come with me when
I go to Chinon?'

'Of course you know that goes without
saying.'

16

Margaret and Louis XI of France finally met towards the end of May in his castle of Chinon. This fortress, standing high above the Vienne some miles before that river mingled with the Loire, had witnessed the death of Henry II of England and the impassioned plea of Joan of Arc that she might be allowed to serve her country. Margaret thought as she waited within its thick walls for Louis to receive her that she must prove herself as staunch a fighter as either of these predecessors.

After much procrastination and haggling, Louis finally agreed to make a gift of twenty thousand livres to his cousin and equip her with an army which was to be led by Pierre. The King of France took three months to come to this decision and Margaret had the arrival of ambassadors from Edward of York to thank for Louis' eventual present. Embarrassed with the prospect of Margaret coming face to face with supporters of her arch enemy he hastily made the award and bid her farewell.

But Louis was not the man to give anything

for nothing and Margaret left behind her a signed treaty in which she agreed to hand over to Louis the English stronghold of Calais. Louis was cunning enough to gloss this tremendous sacrifice by assuring Margaret that he still regarded Henry as the true King of France — he had been crowned, had he not, by Cardinal Beaufort in Notre Dame — and Louis, as Henry's vassal, would simply hold Calais until such time as the Lancastrians had been restored to power.

Jasper, who had joined Margaret with Henry's treasurer for part of the discussions, was to effect the handing over and he remained to conclude the details with Louis.

After visiting René once more in Angers Margaret and Pierre with an army of two thousand well-trained men set out from Normandy for the Tyne.

From the outset the weather was bad and gales and rainstorms lashed the fifty-two small ships of Margaret's fleet. She was, however, so overjoyed at the prospect of Pierre helping her recover Henry's throne that she hardly noticed the inconvenience of heaving decks and constant dampness. Pierre and she spent hours each day in the open air scanning the grey horizons for any of the ships which their spies had told them Edward had ordered into the Channel to waylay them;

but if the mountainous seas were unpleasant they also kept the enemy navy in harbour.

The months of arguing and pleading with the cold and difficult Louis had served to deepen the friendship between the seasoned soldier and the dauntless queen. If Margaret loved him she knew, at least, that if he did not declare his passion he was extremely fond of her and unstinting in his encouragement. There had been moments when dancing together at Chinon or walking in the woods about the castle she had known that she had but to touch his face or put her head upon his shoulder and he would have responded by taking her in his arms and kissing her as she desired. She was at a loss to know why he had made no move and could only conjecture that it was because he knew she had cuckolded Henry. Perhaps it was enough, at this moment, to be embarking on a campaign together. There would be time enough for jubilation later.

At the outset it certainly appeared that success was to crown Margaret's bold venture into her enemy's territory for Brézé and his armies succeeded in taking the Northumbrian castles of Bamborough, Alnwick and Dunstanborough: these were quickly garrisoned. Margaret took up residence in the castle of Bamborough which stood high on a mound overlooking a long beach of sand dunes. Since the time of the Votadini Bamborough had been a stronghold of the Britons and now its battlements were manned night and day with the soldiers of an English queen: Margaret often walked among them cheering them with promises of the riches that would be theirs when Henry was restored to the throne.

Margaret made her headquarters in the Faire Chamber which had a large ante room leading into the Great Hall. Here she sat with Sir Ralph Grey, the commander of the castle, making lists of possible Lancastrian supporters in the neighbourhood and writing letters to Jasper Tudor and other loyal lords begging them to come to her aid as quickly as they could through enemy territory. While she was engaged upon this task Pierre set about strengthening the defences of the ancient stronghold and sending spies out into nearby villages and towns for news of any Yorkist troops.

It was through one of Pierre's most trusted scouts that they heard Warwick was heading northwards in command of an army that some said numbered close on ten thousand. Margaret received this unwelcome information at the end of a disappointing day in which she had interviewed several of the smaller landowners close to Bamborough whom Ralph Grey had assured her were only too anxious to see the return of Henry to the throne but who had been evasive in their offers of help.

'They are afraid to venture forth when our army is so meagre,' Margaret was saying to Grey in a flat voice when Pierre came into the Faire Chamber and told her that Warwick was less than two days' march away.

'What shall we do now?' she asked, putting her hand to her mouth in a gesture which Pierre recognised as one of well-suppressed fear.

'We are provisioned for a long stay here,' Ralph Grey said.

'But we cannot remain, separated from Henry and my son, to be caught like rats in a trap.'

'No, I agree,' Pierre said slowly, 'for our first objective must be to raise more troops and our only hope of doing that seems to be to go to Scotland and find who remains sympathetic to the queen's cause.'

'Then had we not better leave at once while the French fleet is so close? That will give Sir Ralph time to make his plans to withstand a siege if and when Warwick arrives.'

It did not take Margaret very long to gather together her few jewels and a bundle of clothing and thanking Sir Ralph for his welcome and assistance she walked through the inner ward to rejoin Pierre.

As they clambered down the steep, craggy path to the village of Bamborough a sudden and violent gust of wind blew Margaret's hood from her head. A few minutes later it began to rain and by the time they had come to the little harbour close by the mill it was lashing down from a sombre and threatening sky.

Tied to the quay was a fishing boat and one of the three men on board helped Margaret and showed her to the only shelter beneath a half-deck. She huddled here while Pierre and the seamen discussed their destination and haggled over the extra money demanded for putting to sea in such foul weather.

Pierre had brought blankets and some bread and wine; they ate and drank while they were in the comparative calm of the small harbour. Once out in the open sea between the Farne Islands the sea was whipped into a mass of turbulent grey waters by the force of the wind and the rain fell in unrelenting torrents. The seamen, hanging on to the tiller or controlling recalcitrant sails, muttered broad oaths in their Northumbrian dialect. Margaret, mercifully, could not understand more than half of what they said but she was glad when darkness fell and the brief November day was over and Pierre came to sit beside her.

'We could not have picked a worse moment to leave,' she said, huddling against him.

'I do not need to ask if you are afraid.'

'Not with you here, but I fear for the other ships. Are your French captains used to such appalling weather?'

'I am sure they are but I'll admit that I have never put to sea in a storm to equal this.'

'If we do not make the Scottish mainland it will at least be an end to my troubles.'

'You must not speak like that — what would Henry do without you to champion him?'

'Ah, Henry; perhaps he would be better off left to live his life in peace. How do I know that I do the right thing in bringing dissension to this land?'

'You do not bring it for it has been festering for years. Now, come, try to rest.'

Margaret leaned against him, her head on his shoulder, the violent motion of the small fishing vessel now shutting out everything but the comfort of Pierre's closeness. Forgotten now were pride or shame or any other emotion and when he put his arms about her, murmuring her name, she turned towards him with the trusting dependence of a child.

For all she cared the ship might founder; there could be no better way to die.

★ ★ ★

At Berwick, where the seamen thankfully brought the ship into harbour, Margaret and Pierre anxiously awaited the arrival of the French fleet. By nightfall they were saddened by the news brought to them by the battered crews who had managed the passage that four or more of the ships had sank.

'With all hands lost?' Margaret cried.

'It was impossible to go about and pick up survivors but it is rumoured that some men were able to swim ashore to Lindisfarne,' a captain of arms replied.

Margaret and Pierre spent the following day at Berwick hoping for better tidings and for the arrival of the ship in which all the treasure which Louis had given her had been stowed. They were still anxiously waiting that evening when Margaret realised, with despair, that this ship was among those which had foundered. This disaster, coupled with the fact that the masters totalled four hundred men drowned, did not seem a happy omen for her arrival in Scotland. When, some two days later, still waiting in the vain hope that the golden coins and plate might yet be discovered the last blow was dealt when Margaret learnt that Somerset had gone over to the Yorkists, surrendering Bamborough and Dunstanborough as he did so.

'Can we trust no one?' Margaret asked bitterly.

'At least my son seems to be holding out in Alnwick,' Pierre said, making an effort to comfort her and cheering himself at the same time. He had been somewhat against bringing his heir, who had recently married the young daughter of the late King of France and his mistress Agnes Sorel, but Louis had thought it good to blood the young man and such was Pierre's relationship with the French king that he had not considered it wise to cross him. 'As soon as we reach Edinburgh we shall start making plans to relieve Alnwick and recapture Bamborough,' he told her as they set out at last for the Scottish capital.

It was an orderly army that encamped outside the house of Holyrood and Pierre gave the strictest orders to his captains that there should be no pillaging among the narrow wynds of the city. Margaret's hopes of raising Scottish sympathy were so slender that unruly behaviour by his troops might well swing the balance against them.

Within the palace which had been built for Jane Beaufort when she had married James I

265

of Scotland Margaret was reunited with Henry and her son. Henry was touchingly delighted to see her and Margaret was glad to note he appeared to be in better health than when she had left him some six months earlier.

Edward, Prince of Wales, had grown a full three inches in this time and although he was as pleased as Henry to welcome his mother he hid his pleasure in a new-found manliness. He was ready to prattle by the hour of his skill at the butts or the quintain and Pierre soon found a veteran of the French wars willing to improve the boy's skill.

Margaret was not long in discovering that she was even less welcome at the Scottish court than she had been on her previous visit and only the Earl of Angus seemed willing to raise men and lend them money. Most of the Scottish nobles seemed inclined to recognise the Yorkist usurper and Margaret became sickened of listening to the tales of the brilliant court which Edward kept in Windsor and the other English castles which belonged, by right, to Henry and herself. She grieved most over Greenwich where Edward delighted to sport with whichever pretty woman was attracting his amorous fancies. It was only slightly comforting to be told that Edward did not really enjoy the war-making which Warwick insisted was necessary to keep a hold on the throne.

'He would be content to pass his time in dalliance while his cousin fought for him,' Angus told Pierre and Margaret.

'Who would not?' Pierre said lightly and for a fraction of a second he and Margaret looked at one another before they returned to the important task of counting the number of troops who could be relied upon to follow the Lancastrian banner into England.

* * *

At last, despite the opposition of the queen mother of Scotland who considered Margaret's chance to be very slim, Pierre gathered together about ten thousand men. This army set out earlier than it should have done when news came to Margaret that Louis was preparing to settle his age-old differences with England in a meeting arranged for the two monarchs by Philip of Burgundy.

The Lancastrian army, made up largely of Scots and Frenchmen, led by de Brézé and with Margaret, Henry and the young prince in its train met with initial success. The Northumberland castles whose captains did not receive the rewards they had been promised by Edward let down their drawbridges and once again Margaret entered Bamborough. Not so successful was an attack upon Norham Castle in which Margaret accompanied her soldiers, hoping by her presence to fan the small glimmer of hope which the taking of the other strongholds had engendered. While the Lancastrian army fell back on Bamborough Warwick, smarting under the reverse he had suffered, brought fresh troops and his splendid young king to recover the place.

Stealthily the Scots and the French began to disappear from the Lancastrian army and each day brought news of skirmishes in which Warwick had cut fleeing troops to pieces.

'We cannot sustain such losses,' Pierre told Margaret as they stood on the battlements anxiously scrutinising the distant Cheviots for the sight of an approaching army.

'My advice is to leave again while there is still a hope of seeking help elsewhere,' Sir Ralph Grey said, coming up from the keep staircase in time to hear this statement.

'But there is nowhere to go,' Margaret replied. 'I refuse to go again to Scotland where Margaret of Gueldres appears to be bewitched with the success of Edward and Warwick and I utterly refuse to crawl to cousin Louis. It is impossible to know what that man is thinking and, with this conference pending to make peace with Edward, I can but assume that he is like the queen mother of Scotland and is in thrall to the usurper.'

'Then I can only suggest that as Philip of Burgundy appears to be the key man in the conciliation you should appeal to him.'

'But he has never had time for me, Pierre.'

'Charles has, though; he never forgets that he has a grandmother who was a daughter of John of Gaunt and always favours the Lancastrians.'

'You think he might be persuaded to induce his father to help me?'

'Why not? Even if your presence in Flanders serves to disrupt the conference you will have accomplished a great deal.'

'Then we shall go.' Margaret was never slow to make up her mind. 'But his grace, will he be safe here?'

'I shall lay down my life to ensure his safety,' Grey said earnestly. 'You may depend upon me.'

As it was the only reasonable thing Margaret could do she reluctantly set about making plans to quit the castle and sail for Flanders.

Henry, who seemed quite happy to remain within the solid walls of Bamborough, begged Margaret to stay with him. 'I am sure that my brother Jasper will in time be able to raise enough loyal people to rescue us and what shall I do with you away from me?'

'It will not be for long,' Margaret consoled him. 'You will see that before the year is out I shall return again with Burgundian gold this time. We must have more money if we are to continue the struggle; even if Jasper succeeds in raising an army it has to be fed and paid. Try to occupy yourself in ruling this tiny part of England which is still yours and I shall be back before you have noticed that I have gone.'

'You are a courageous woman, my dear, and I shall do what you say. God speed your talks with Burgundy and may they meet with the success they deserve.' He smiled at her, the sweet, trusting smile that he reserved only for her. For a moment Margaret's iron will deserted her and tears filled her eyes.

'Take good care of yourself, Henry, and see that that lazy servant of yours washes your linen and keeps a stock of warm clothing for the winter ahead. Write to me as I shall to you and pray that we may soon be together again. I shall not rest until I have exhausted every possible source of help. Now, be of good heart, and bid me farewell.' She stooped to kiss him as she would a weakly and gentle child, yearning over his helplessness like an anxious mother. Henry clung to her and only with difficulty was she able to disentangle herself and walk resolutely from the room. She waited on the stone stairway while Edward, who was to sail with her, came to make his farewells to Henry; it was too much to bear to witness the parting of her son and her husband.

She was not to know that they were never to meet again.

* * *

Margaret hardly spoke as she rejoined Pierre, Exeter, Sir John and Lady Fortescue who were to travel with her and Edward to Flanders. In silence the party, accompanied by the faithful Rose and three other serving women, walked down the steep and craggy path to the harbour beside the mill. To Margaret it seemed only a short while since she had boarded the fishing vessel and had been caught up in the ferocious storm which had done more than anything to rob her of a possible homecoming as the wife of a restored Henry.

Now Pierre and Margaret embarked on one of the four balingers placed at their disposal while Exeter, Edward and Sir John Fortescue, who was to act as the boy's tutor, went to another.

The weather was totally different from the tempest which had whipped the seas to fury in the previous November and now the sun shone on calm waters. Margaret stayed at the rail while they threaded their way through the scattered islands of Farne until Bamborough was a pale shadow on the distant horizon. Pierre came to stand beside her in companionable silence until she spoke to him without looking at him.

'How may I ever repay you for all that you have done for Henry and for me?'

'I have failed you in so many ways that I do not think the question arises. I ask myself what I can still do for you in the future. I wonder perhaps if you were to replace me as your general you might find Louis more amenable; it is possible that he still bears me a grudge for that old allegiance I had to his father against him when he was Dauphin.'

'If you leave me I shall give up the struggle.' Margaret put up a hand to catch a strand of hair which blew in the soft summer air. 'Do you want to leave me, Pierre?'

'You know I would rather be with you than anywhere else on earth.'

'Thank you for that and for so much else; without you I should not have been able to leave money to feed Henry and his little court. Do you know that I have but ten florins in the pouch at my waist? And you gave me those.'

'Do not worry about money at this moment. I shall not let you or your followers starve when we land in Flanders and I'll even scrape the coffers to see if we can find funds to provide you with a new gown or two. Becoming as you are to me in that dress you must be heartily tired of wearing it day after day.' His smile took the sting out of the words and she laughed; a mirthless sound which ended on a sigh.

'Oh, Pierre, I have erred somewhere so very much. Have I been too warlike for a woman and the fates punish me?'

'Of course not, you have fought only for your own and I believe you are the bravest woman in the world.' He put his hand over hers as it lay on the rail. 'I wish to God that you and I were floating down the Loire with a day of pleasure before us when we might talk of other matters but the amassing of an army or the placating of overproud rulers.'

'Life does not intend that I shall ever be happy or at peace.'

'You must not say that for it tempts providence. Try not to think of the past but enjoy this moment and in that way you will be made ready to set about the formidable task of winning Philip of Burgundy to our side.'

* * *

When the forlorn band arrived at Sluys without a change of raiment between them Pierre found them a quiet lodging house and Margaret, anxious to lose no time, sent a messenger to Philip requesting an audience.

While she waited in barely concealed impatience for his reply she visited the merchants' houses with Edward and bought for him and herself a few articles of clothing. Pierre had generously given her money for this and she was forced to accept his charity. It might be wise to appear not to be affluent when she came at last to Philip's court but he might scoff at the threadbare gown which was the only dress in her wardrobe.

After several days Philip sent one of his most skilled statesmen to the Queen of England to tell her that he regretted it was not possible to receive her.

'But I have been instructed by my husband to insist that I see your noble master,' Margaret told the ambassador with great dignity and emphasis. This was partly true and the thought gave her courage.

'My master much regrets that he cannot

give you an audience because he is engaged upon business of the most important nature.' Such as giving away my kingdom to my rival, Margaret thought bitterly. 'He is so very sorry and trusts that your father will come to your aid.' The man was courteous but adamant and after a few more polite exchanges Margaret dismissed him.

'Let us seek out Charles,' she said to de Brézé when he rejoined her after escorting the Burgundian to the door.

'Tomorrow?' Pierre asked.

'Now,' Margaret answered.

So Pierre paid their dues at the lodging-house, hired horses for the party and they set out for Bruges where Charles kept a court which rivalled that of his father in its splendour.

Here, Charles, Count of Charolais, received Margaret and her handful of faithful followers with more kindness than she had had for months. Charles that quarrelsome and fiery young man, went out of his way to provide the unfortunate Queen of England with entertainment which was like balm to her weary spirit. In the most splendidly appointed rooms hung with priceless tapes-tries and furnished with exquisite taste Margaret relaxed with Pierre and her other friends and enjoyed good food and excellent wines. More important than the lavish hospitality was Charles' success in obtaining for Margaret an interview with his father.

'You must humour him, cousin, for he grows old; this Crusade that he preaches is only an attempt to recapture some of his ancient glory. Now that he finds his charming mistresses a little more than he can manage he has to appear to be occupied with the world's affairs. Although, I must admit that he has lost some of his enthusiasm for restoring the Middle East to Christianity since King Louis has persuaded him to act as mediator in this conference which is taking place at St. Omer. My good father can think of nothing but making a lasting peace between France and England.'

'And Louis overlooks me in his haste to make friends with Edward and Warwick,' Margaret stated, flatly.

'I'm afraid that is so.'

'Then it is more important than ever that I should see your father at once.'

'But he is at St. Pol, which is but a stone's throw from Béthune and the English garrison at Calais.'

'I shall travel in disguise and no English soldier, however quick-witted, would think to see his dethroned queen bringing vegetables to market in a farm wagon.'

It was Pierre who found the covered cart; but he would not allow her to take upon herself the role of a peasant. 'I'm going with you and you must take two or three of your women as well; it would be foolish to try and act a part, but dressed simply as you are, you would easily pass for a poor lady travelling with her husband and attendants.'

'Very well,' she agreed; but she did not look at him.

Thanking Charles for his kindness they left the peaceful canal-ribboned city of Bruges to the sound of church bells at first light on the following morning. They were soon mingling with the crowds on their way to and from the market with produce and once on the sun-baked road made good time. It was a still evening, with the summer sun setting in their faces, as they came into Courtrai.

Here Pierre drove the cart with its canvas-covered tilt into the yard of the best inn of the Grand Place. Throwing the reins to an ostler he jumped from the driving seat. 'Wait here while I procure you the best accommodation the place has to offer,' he said, smiling.

Stiff with the sitting and the jolting of the springless cart Margaret, Rose and another maid climbed down and walked in the cobbled courtyard.

Pierre reappeared to announce that he had been fortunate enough to find rooms for them all and had ordered hot water for Margaret to bath.

Later, when she had washed off the dirt of the day's travelling and had put on again the dress which Rose had taken outside and beaten, Pierre came to her room. It was dark now and candles glimmered against the panelling.

'You and I are going to eat here, in peace, while Rose and the girl can go downstairs. The host tells me there is a mummers' troupe coming to give a play in the Place soon and they can watch that. Do you mind that I have taken so much upon myself?'

'You know that I do not.' Margaret stood at the open window, refreshed and forgetful of all else but the fact that she and Pierre were alone. He came to stand beside her, carrying goblets of wine. As she leant against the casement he put up his hand and touched her cheek. Margaret turned her face and kissed the palm of his hand. 'I love you, Pierre de Brézé,' she said, unsteadily, at last.

'And I you, Margaret of Anjou.'

17

Philip the Good relented sufficiently to send archers to Béthune to bring Margaret and Pierre to him in safety. At St. Pol, de Brézé pleaded her cause so skilfully with the ageing but most powerful duke in France that Margaret and he were given large sums of money and a banquet in the true tradition of Burgundian hospitality.

On the day immediately following this gargantuan feast Philip made his excuses to the English queen and went on his way.

'He has left his sister to entertain you,' Pierre consoled her, 'although I recognise that as the sop for which it is.'

'He is sorry for me, as most men are, but none of them want to commit themselves to my hopeless cause. What shall I do now?'

'We had better return to Bruges and see what comes out of the meeting at St. Omer.'

In the sadness of her later life Margaret was to look back on these two weeks she spent with Pierre as the only really happy time a relentless fate allowed. Staunch friends and allies in public, they were lovers in secret; Margaret discovering in this man whom she had loved and admired for so long a miraculous sense of fulfilment and completion. Both knew that when once they returned to Bruges they would be forced to return to the platonic relationship which had been theirs over the past years but were willing to pay this price for their escape into another world.

It was this sense of underlying happiness which sustained Margaret as she heard the results of the St. Omer meeting and knew that Edward with Warwick at his elbow was convincing his fellow monarch that Louis must forget the Lancastrians and believe in Edward's friendship. Margaret's only comfort was the fact that although marriages between either Louis' daughter or sister-in-law and Edward were mooted they went no further. Yet what did royal marriages signify when all was said and done? Had she not been sacrificed in vain?

By Christmas Margaret realised that she could no longer live upon Charles' hospitality in Bruges. Pierre went to Angers and to Chinon and returned with an offer of a tiny pension and the use of René's house in St. Mihiel close to her birthplace at Pont-à-Mousson. Reluctantly Margaret agreed to accept the offer and live quietly while her friends still in England worked to restore

Henry to his throne. She could do no more.

'I shall have to return to my estates,' Pierre told her, 'for Louis told me that I had had sufficient leave of absence.'

'He seeks to take away my final prop.'

'But I shall never desert you and will come to you from the ends of the earth should you call. If everyone else has failed you I promise that I shall not.'

'And I believe you.'

When the time came to go to St. Mihiel Pierre escorted them and they were joined by Exeter who brought them news of Henry who lived quietly in Bamborough in the company of those Lancastrians who managed to evade the constant vigil of Warwick and his Neville relations.

'There is no hope of a rising in our favour anywhere in the realm?' Margaret asked him.

'None, your grace,' Exeter told her heavily.

'So be it, I must stay here and hope God will aid us.'

Pierre remained three days at the small house close to the church in St. Mihiel then came to Margaret to announce that he was leaving almost at once.

'It is better that I go quickly; and, after all, we have been separated before.'

'Yes, but not in this fashion. Yet I shall not weep or make protestation for I would not want you to remember me with a tear-sodden face.' There would be plenty of time for weeping when he was gone.

She clung to him when he stooped to kiss her and then pushed him away, turning to pick up a rolled document from a nearby table. 'Be gone,' she said loudly, 'be gone.'

In a torment of grief she threw herself into the management of her small household, finding extra tutors for her son and merchants who would provide her with the barest necessities at the lowest possible prices. It was a challenge to her energy and ability and she used it to allay her endless misery.

Soon after Easter she heard that a Lancastrian army under the command of Somerset, who had once more returned to his true loyalty, was about to launch an attack in the north of England. Hardly able to believe that the wheel of fortune might be turning in her direction she made tentative arrangements to leave St. Mihiel should it be necessary.

Within a few short weeks she knew that the army had been utterly defeated at Hexham and the Duke of Somerset had lost his head. Warwick had not forgotten the fate of his own father. Henry had escaped from Bamborough, but no one knew his whereabouts. Utterly dejected by this disappointing news

Margaret heard in a letter from Pierre, who was kept constantly on Louis' business of placating his rebellious lords, that Warwick was coming to France to make arrangements with the French King for the marriage of Edward with Bona of Savoy.

'Do not worry overmuch about the matter for it has not happened as yet and Louis has enough on his hands with the Burgundians who cannot forgive him for taking back Picardy. Though I think he brings much on himself, I am almost sorry for Louis. Even your father is not such a good friend since Louis would not aid you — and who could blame him for that? Our King of France is of a stamp I have never before encountered; he means to have complete dominance and he goes about his business like a spider spinning his web. His ways are not mine and I doubt if they are much to the liking of the Dukes of Brittany and Burgundy — have you heard that there had been a plot upon the life of Charles of Charolais and it is being openly said that Louis might be implicated? I am a man of action myself but there is a time for making war and another for peaceful dalliance. Do you think he can ever have loved a woman as I do you?'

Pierre's wise counsel proved more accurate than he realised and Margaret was to be glad that she had not wasted a great deal of time in worrying about the marriage of Edward of England to a French princess. For while Louis waited — as only he could when he wanted something — for Warwick to come to France and sign the formal contract it was to appear that he waited in vain. Warwick was not coming and for the very good reason that his king had fallen in love with Elizabeth Grey, who had once been Margaret's lady in waiting, and had married her secretly. Warwick, it was reported to the court at St. Milhiel by pedlars who had it from merchants who had it from seafarers, was in a towering rage with his protégé and sulked in his castle.

By the same means Margaret heard the most conflicting rumours of Henry's movements and for one period during the bleak autumn of 1464 mourned his death. This unhappy rumour was scotched when a letter was brought to her smuggled from the wilds of Ribblesdale in England and written by Henry himself. He told her that he was in hiding with good friends and was well cared for; his daily prayer was that she and their son were alive and in good health.

This most welcome surprise caused Margaret to celebrate Christmas with more cheer than she would have done and to drink a toast to the bride of Edward who had done much to dismay his Yorkist following. Any crumb of comfort was good in times as hard as those which Margaret suffered at this moment.

This winter was perhaps the coldest within living memory and when Louis and his nobles left Tours after a meeting designed to put an end to the rumours that they were plotting his downfall the great rivers of France were frozen over and Margaret and her little court put on all the clothing they possessed in an effort to keep out the swingeing cold.

One day in late February when there seemed no sign of a break in the relentless cold Margaret was sitting by a small stove pushing frozen fingers to write a letter to the King of Portugal in the faint hope of enlisting his sympathy. She was sitting back, frowning, when Rose came to say that Monsieur le Comte de Brézé requested an audience.

'I cannot believe it!' Margaret cried as Pierre followed the girl into the room. 'I must be dreaming.'

'Indeed you are not, and I have been trying for an age to come to you. Only Louis could have kept me away and he is more demanding than ever just now; I am convinced that his nobles are conspiring against him and I do not know if he feigns indifference or not. But

I do not come to talk of him but to see you and find out how you fare. Is this the best you can do for warmth?'

'It is well enough and I am so happy that you are come that I do not feel the cold. Let me give you some wine and food and then you can tell me all the gossip of the world since last we met.'

Pierre stayed with her for a week and saw to it that she was able to buy extra wood for the stove and more food; he took Edward riding in the forests around Bar-le-duc and replenished the larder with the spoils of their hawking and archery.

But best of all he sat with Margaret deep into the night talking of the hundred and one subjects which bound them together. They lamented the fate of Somerset and the other Lancastrian rebels, gloated over Warwick's discomfort and hoped that Henry might stay safely hidden.

When the time came for him to depart Margaret could not believe that a week had passed so quickly. She wept openly as he bade her farewell and all his promises of coming soon again could not console her. When she had watched his horse disappear along the road for Paris she retired to her chamber and refused entry to anyone until the following day. She was so downcast that she wondered if it might have been better if he had stayed away; at least she had become almost used to living without him but this reunion only served to open the wound.

With her usual resilience she recovered after a while and took up again those activities upon which she had been engaged before he came. The letter to Alfonso of Portugal was redrafted, finished and despatched and she set about the task of making herself a dress from some woollen stuff Pierre had brought her as a present. There was nothing she could do but wait for news and the quickest way to go mad was to be idle.

By Easter all of France knew that the king was making preparation to go against those of his nobles who had been misguided enough to line themselves up behind his young brother and plot to overthrow him.

'Are the realms of this world never to be at peace?' Margaret asked Exeter one morning as she received a letter from her father in which he said he was just about to depart for Saumur to join the king.

'It would appear to be well nigh impossible,' Exeter said shaking his head.

And it certainly seemed so during the early summer when Burgundy, Brittany and the king's brother gathered huge armies together and at last showed their hand by

287

advancing on Paris.

Louis, entrusting the command of his army to the only man who remained loyal throughout this difficult spring, put Pierre in the advance guard. He rode out to face the masse strength of Charles of Charolais, who not so long before had played host to him and Margaret in Bruges.

In St. Mihiel Margaret found the summer heat overpowering; she was restless and ill at ease while she wondered if battle had been enjoined between the king and his wayward brother. Trying to take her mind from the prospect of war she rode with Edward and the others on day-long excursions which left her physically exhausted and saddle weary. She longed for news of Pierre and watched the dusty roads for signs of messengers with letters.

Not until the end of July did a squire of René's come to the chateau and when he came he asked not for Margaret but for the Duke of Exeter.

Exeter received him in the anteroom next to the salon. 'You are from René, Duke of Anjou?'

'I am, my lord and it was his express wish that I saw you first — '

'You bring bad news?' Exeter asked sharply.

'Of a great battle by the king's army and of the death of Monsieur le Comte de Brézé.'

'Oh, no,' Exeter said, 'I do not think that my mistress will be able to sustain such a blow. Ye gods, has she not suffered enough already that she could not have been spared this? I ask you, what has she done to deserve such treatment? Go and refresh yourself and I will think how I may best break this news.'

When he found sufficient courage to go into Margaret he found her on her knees in her salon pouring over a map of Paris and its environs. She looked up at Exeter as he entered and her face was pale as moonlight on a pool, her eyes black and enormous. 'You can only come to me looking like that, Exeter, when you are afraid to speak. Don't keep me waiting, I implore you. Is it Henry or — '

'Your grace, it is the Sire de Brézé.'

Margaret's hand went to her mouth and the already dilated pupils widened; she asked in a flat, expressionless voice: 'Where?'

'Montlhéry.'

'Oh, God!' Margaret threw herself across the parchment map and Exeter thought for a moment that she had fainted but when he moved towards her she stirred. 'Send someone to Paris and find out what happened.'

Hurrying to obey Exeter thought it would

have been better if she had been overcome with tears. This calm presaged more trouble than a paroxysm of weeping.

The tears did not come until Fortescue came back with a description of Pierre's bravery in the battle. Margaret would not be spared any detail and listened in silence to a description of the drawing up of the French cavalry to face the enemy, the defiant peal of Pierre's trumpeters and the charge which he led into the thick of the Burgundian horsemen. For an hour or more he cut and hacked his way through the snorting and rearing horses his sword in his hand until he was alone in a spearhead. Surrounded on all sides he was an easy target and was put to death.

'He did not die in vain,' Fortescue continued bravely in the face of Margaret's calm, 'for his leadership set the pattern of the day's fighting.'

'And his body?'

'Recovered for decent burial. It is said, my lady, that the King of France is most bitterly grieved for the loss of his friend and ours.'

'What does he know of grief?'

Margaret rose from the chair on which she had sat down to listen to Fortescue and retired to her room. By the late evening, when she did not reappear all the household were exceedingly anxious. Rose volunteered to run the risk of Margaret's anger at being disturbed and timidly knocked upon her door. When she did not receive an answer she ventured into the room and found her mistress, fully dressed, lying face down on her bed, asleep.

Margaret returned to her anxious household during the morning of the following day but it was soon plain that she was in the grip of some fever. Lady Fortescue managed to persuade her to return to bed where she allowed herself to be undressed. She drank some cooling elixir which was always kept in the stillroom to relieve distress while the physician from the village was hastily summoned.

It took Margaret ten days to recover from her illness and when she emerged from the sick room and called for her household books she was emaciated and wan. Exeter, coming to pay his respects, found her changed and old. He knew better than to commiserate with her and told her instead of a merchant he had discovered who would undertake to keep the household in wax for their candles and tapers for a price considerably less than they had paid before.

She took up the detail of household management as if it were the most important matter in the world while her heart continued to break within her breast.

* * *

When she heard, before the next Christmas-tide, that Henry had eventually been captured and led as a captive to the Tower of London she made only one comment. 'I am a sinner and God has seen fit to punish me; we are born to suffer and to pay the price of our misdemeanours.'

18

'You may tell his highness the King of France that I do not accept his invitation.' Margaret's voice as she stood at the window of the chateau at St. Mihiel was cold.

'But, madame, King Louis commands — '

'Commands the Queen of England? You speak without thinking. You may tell your master that I have no intention of committing my folly of two years ago and come hastening to his bidding only to find myself rejected and made to look a fool.'

'There is no question of such a thing happening again; his highness bids you as his honoured guest to come to him at Amboise.'

It was now the summer of 1470. Margaret had not changed very much since the fateful time when she had been told of Pierre's death; lack of rich food had kept her figure trim and she still moved with characteristic grace. Close examination, however, betrayed that fine lines creased the corner of her eyes and white strands mingled in her abundant hair.

'There is hope now that my master will be able to offer you real help as well as hospitality,' the French ambassador pleaded. He began to feel irritated with this implacable Angevin woman and did not relish the thought of returning to Louis with her refusal.

'Good sir, during the last twenty-odd years I have been offered assistance only when what I had to give was more valuable than what I was about to receive.'

'But, my lady, the Sire de Brézé would have laid down his life in your service — '

'How dare you speak of matters of which you have no knowledge? This interview is at an end; perhaps I shall feel more disposed to listen to you tomorrow.'

To tell the truth she had a headache which refused to leave her and the man's manner and voice irritated her. When he had gone she rang her silver handbell for Rose and asked her bring her the juice of some of their precious store of lemons mixed with water and sugar.

She sat drinking this in the cool draught of air from the open window; not hearing the soft cooing of the ring doves in the lime trees or the constant twitter of the myriad grasshoppers. The years since Pierre had died had been a succession of dull days enlivened from time to time by attempts to raise some spark of enthusiasm for her plight in one of the monarchs of Europe.

One of the better moments of her virtual imprisonment had been the arrival of Jasper Tudor in St. Mihiel. Unlike those about who had become resigned to their non-combatant roles he was full of enthusiasm for his half-brother's restoration. Since she had last seen him in Northumberland he had been attainted, as had all the Lancastrians, and had lived in a Welsh mountain retreat where he worked unceasingly to further Henry's interest. His sister-in-law, Margaret Beaufort, had now married the second son of the late Duke of Buckingham, Henry Stafford, and lived quietly on her estates. His young nephew had been put in the charge of William Herbert who had been appointed Earl of Pembroke in Jasper's place.

'Do you not miss your nephew and his mother?' Margaret asked him.

'I do, more than I can tell you; but I think you understand what it is to lose those that we love'

Was the remark intended to mean Henry or did Jasper guess that Pierre de Brézé had been the love of her life? She could not be sure for Jasper had a certain quality of character, derived no doubt from his mixture of Welsh and French blood, which was enigmatic. There was more to him than

295

courage and hard work.

It was Jasper who fostered that Lancastrian plot which was hatched in 1468, when Margaret had travelled as far as Normandy to await a return to England. This had been most successful at first but had gone no further than Wales and had been defeated in the end. It was this episode and Margaret's readiness to join the fight once more which had won Louis' grudging approval and made him less inclined than before to aid her rival in England. At least, Margaret comforted herself that this was the case; there were those who plainly stated that Louis had finished with Edward and the Yorkists from the moment that Charles, now Duke of Burgundy, had married Edward's sister and thus cemented the Anglo-Burgundian alliance. Jasper had much to tell Margaret of the magnificence of this splendid wedding and he had taken some of the smart out of the withdrawal of Charles' friendship by assuring her that he would rather have the King of France on his side than the rash and bad-tempered duke.

Yet of all the news that Jasper brought to her little court in exile the most welcome was the growing rift between Warwick and his puppet king.

'You have no idea how things have changed

at court since the early days,' Jasper told her, 'I have it on the best of authority that Warwick hardly knows how to be civil to Edward.'

'But I cannot understand the reason for this change of heart.'

'It is quite simple, Margaret. Edward's queen was born a Woodville and that family is the most ambitious in England; more so even than the Nevilles, if you can believe it. Elizabeth, as you remember, was the eldest daughter of the seven children born to Sir Richard, now Earl Rivers, and his wife the widow of Bedford, Henry's uncle. Since Edward's secret marriage Elizabeth has done all she can to promote the advancement of her brothers and sisters and has succeeded so well that the Nevilles are right out of favour. Of course, Edward had a motive in complying with his wife's wishes for he must be afraid of Warwick and the power which he wielded in the land.'

'Is he as powerful today?'

'Impossible to say but I believe he courts the favour of Edward's brother Clarence in an effort to keep his influence upon the royal household.'

'What of Richard of Gloucester, Edward's other brother?'

'He is devoted to Edward and follows him

like the man's shadow.'

At this moment as Margaret sipped the cooling drink Jasper was not at St. Mihiel for she had sent him to the Loire to see René and ask her father if the signs she had had recently of Louis' returning friendship might be relied upon or not. Margaret missed her brother-in-law for he was a wonderful teller of stories and had entertained them throughout the long winter evenings when they had tired of card games and other distractions.

Thinking of him now she made up her mind to keep Louis' messenger waiting until Jasper returned. This decision made she felt happier in her mind and went to seek out her son who was at his studies with Sir John; she felt the need of exercise and Edward, now a well-grown youth of sixteen, enjoyed a hawking expedition as much as she.

* * *

Jasper returned in the following week during which time Margaret had gone out of her way to charm the French ambassador; it was one thing to play the haughty queen and feel that all power had not been stripped from her but another to bite the only friendly hand which had been extended to her in recent years. After all it was Louis who gave her permission to remain upon French soil.

Jasper came hurrying in to her salon as soon as he had washed off the dust of his swift journey from the Loire and was bursting with news.

'Margaret, the most incredible thing has happened — Warwick is in France!'

'On an embassy from Edward? but I thought he would have sent a Woodville?'

'He is here on no embassy — he comes to seek Louis' aid in pushing Edward from his throne. I just cannot believe it. There he is in Normandy, swearing that he is finished with Edward, with all his family.'

'Is it true?' Margaret asked, hardly able to grasp this astonishing event.

'Perfectly true. I have spoken with men who have met him and what is more Warwick's daughter Isabel is married to Clarence and has given birth to a child. Margaret, you must not delay, you must go to Louis in Amboise as soon as possible; now is the moment we have been waiting for all these years. Can you not see it? If Louis is willing to receive Clarence and Warwick it means that he will stop at nothing to help us topple Edward.' His mobile face was alight with enthusiasm but Margaret still felt some constraint; there was something in this matter which she could not fathom.

'You said that Louis is willing to receive Warwick and Clarence?'

'Yes, immediately.'

'And he asks me to go to Amboise?'

'He is eager to help you, your father assures me.'

'But if Warwick — ' She stopped abruptly. 'Do you mean that it is Louis' intention to bring me face to face with the man who has been the reason for most of the misery in my life? I see it all now, and can understand why his ambassador has been so pressing. Of course I shall not go — I should rather walk into a den of lions.' Her face was suffused in indignant colour.

'But Margaret, you would be throwing away a chance of a lifetime if you did not go to Amboise and see what Louis proposes. Think about it, won't you? Even if it costs you the sinking of your pride, is it not worth it for Henry's sake?'

Now he had touched upon the raw wound of her betrayal of that gentle creature. Reluctantly she agreed to go to Amboise.

This magnificent chateau, set high above the broad Loire, had always been one of her favourite visiting places, but she approached it now with trepidation. Her coming was something of an anti-climax for the dreaded foe of her early life had had to leave precipitately to deal with a fleet of Burgundian ships which had set upon his own anchored in Honfleur. Margaret did not know whether to be glad or sorry.

Louis was apparently delighted to meet her and made much of her and her entourage. He was especially pleased with Margaret's son and congratulated her upon his upbringing and manly bearing. Margaret realised this was a compliment for Louis' new-born heir was sickly and weak.

The King of France lost no time in broaching the matter of Margaret's reconciliation with Warwick.

'Your highness, how can you ask me to become friends with this man who robbed Henry of his throne?'

'He realises the error of his ways and wishes to atone for the hurt he has caused you. He is by no means the tyrant that you would suppose and is a man of culture and some sympathy.'

'I find that extremely difficult to believe,' Margaret retorted.

In the end, however, she consented to go to Angers where in her father's house Louis, René and Warwick might meet and she stay in the background, only emerging if she thought it proper.

She found René as enthusiastic for the

301

alliance between herself and Warwick as was Louis. 'Think of the advantages of having him on your side rather than against you — your armies were never a match for his and he will bring you victory,' her grossly overweight father urged her.

Warwick was still recouping his losses after the Burgundian attack so she was given a small breathing space. Louis returned to the attack, bringing his persuasive powers to bear upon this project which had taken precedence over all others. His puckish delight in putting the cat among the pigeons had never stood in hope of such rewards.

Margaret was flattered by Louis' invitation to Edward to stand as godfather to the long-awaited heir to the French throne and she gladly signed a treaty of truce between herself and France once Henry and she were restored as the rightful English monarchs.

'And you will never sit upon the throne of England, madam, unless my lord Warwick places you there,' Louis admonished her.

So she consented to see her arch enemy when he arrived at Angers and waited for him one summer morning with Sir John Fortescue and Jasper Tudor on her one hand and the King of France and her father on the other. She had never been so nervous in her life.

When Warwick was announced she could

hardly lift her eyes to greet him but saw immediately that he had aged considerably. He had still an air of great distinction and his courtly manners were obvious as he knelt to her in the most abject submission of apology.

She greeted him distantly and kept him on his knees while he poured out his defence of his past actions and promised that he would serve her as loyally in the future as he had been prepared to support Edward.

'Your grace, I have been most foully ill-treated and my friends and I have been deprived of privileges and lands. We desire nothing more than to restore you to your correct place upon the English throne so that all may live in peace once more.'

'How can I trust you, my lord of Warwick?'

'You have but to look at those who will stand surety for me; your own father and his highness the King of France.'

'And you wish me to pardon you for your heinous crimes against my husband and my own person?'

'If you can find it in your generous heart so to do.'

At last she began to feel some slight sympathy for the proud earl as he knelt to her and she somewhat ungraciously agreed to accept his help and his remorse.

While she listened to Warwick's protestation of renewed fealty to her and to Henry, the King of France and René swore on a relic of the True Cross that the Lancastrian cause was now their own.

Later Louis came to Margaret's own apartments in the castle and after congratulating her upon her wisdom in accepting Warwick's submission and help he gently spoke to her of the other matter which Warwick and he had discussed.

'And you will give your consent to the marriage of the Prince of Wales with Anne, Warwick's daughter?'

'No, your highness, I can see no reason for such a match. Is it not sufficient that I have agreed to put my trust in a man who has been my hated enemy for most of my days as queen?'

Louis could not budge her but he was not the man to give in easily and for two weeks he kept his court kicking their heels while he pleaded with Margaret. At last weary of the continual barrage Margaret gave her consent and then only when Louis assured her that without the marriage she had no real hold upon the earl. Margaret now felt strong enough to make her own terms and she stated that she would not allow the prince to cross into England until she took him when she thought the time was ripe and that she must keep the young Anne with her.

Warwick now set about the task of arming his troops at Louis' expense, until in September he set sail for Devon with an escort of French ships and a large army of invasion. Margaret, who had come to admire his purpose but still could not bring herself to like the man, watched him depart and prayed by the hour for the success of his venture.

She had more than a month to wait before the tremendous news of his victory was brought to her. Jasper sent special messengers telling her of Edward's flight to the Netherlands and the restoration of Henry to the throne. All the attainders on the Lancastrians had been reversed and the Yorkists were now on the run.

The envoys told her that Henry had been brought from the Tower and treated with great respect; he had conducted his first Parliament and had been welcomed by thousands of sympathetic Londoners.

Warwick had achieved his success without any bloodshed so well had the Lancastrian plans been laid and even Elizabeth Woodville, who gave birth to her first son at this time, was honourably treated.

'When shall we cross to England?' Edward asked her, his young face alight with the thought to being once more part of a great court.

'When King Louis is certain that the new Parliament in London will honour the treaty that I signed on their behalf,' Margaret told him drily, hiding her own impatience. Although she and her son and new daughter-in-law were costing Louis a great deal of money she knew well enough that he would hold her a virtual hostage until he was satisfied that all his diplomacy had not been in vain.

Just before Christmas Louis bade her farewell and she set out for Paris on the first stage of her homeward journey. In the capital of France she was received with great warmth and she much enjoyed showing her son and the pretty little girl he had married to the rejoicing populace.

As soon as she could possibly leave Paris Margaret set out for Rouen and the Channel port where French ships were waiting to take her through the Burgundian blockade which Edward had persuaded his brother-in-law Charles of Burgundy to mount on his behalf.

In Rouen Margaret left Edward and Anne in the same hostelry in which she had stayed almost ten years earlier on her first visit to importune Louis and went alone to the cathedral.

She had a special reason for this pilgrimage for it was here that Pierre was buried and she wished to pay homage to his memory at the moment of her triumphant return to England. She stayed beside his splendid tomb on her knees until they ached with the effort while she remembered him in the splendour of his manhood and in the quieter hours of their shared love for one another. Sad but strengthened she rejoined her son and those of her court who had remained with her in France and made preparation to embark the following day.

Her fleet sailed to the mouth of the Seine and tied up at the quayside of Honfleur. A few minutes later Sir John Fortescue came to tell her that the master of the ship had been informed as soon as he docked that the Burgundian army was about to invade England in a counter-attack against Warwick.

'Oh, no!' she cried, while tears came into her eyes. 'Then we had best wait until we see for which English port they are heading for we cannot fall foul of them in the Channel where we might be taken prisoner.'

It was a fatal decision.

For several weeks she delayed until she heard, with the greatest possible dismay, that Edward, primed with Burgundian gold, had landed once more in England and was gathering an army to lead against Warwick.

Now she did not hesitate. 'We must sail at once.'

But it seemed as if the fates conspired against her and it was the thirteenth of April before contrary winds would allow her to cross the Channel. She arrived in Weymouth on the fourteenth and with her little party went to Cerne Abbas to await news. She had expected to find Jasper Tudor awaiting her but he had wearied of his vigil and had gone off to Wales to strengthen his own army on Edward's reappearance.

Margaret was not kept long in suspense for on the following day she received the Earl of Devon and other Lancastrian nobles. They brought with them the woeful tale of a great battle fought in the mist at Barnet when Warwick had been killed and his magnificent army vanquished.

Now, that control which had stood Margaret in such good stead over the long years of her vigil deserted her and she broke down and sobbed.

'I am the most unfortunate woman in the world, everything I touch is cursed. Why did I delay? Why were the winds so contrary?'

It was some hours before Devon and his companions were able to convince her that all was not yet lost and that she had many friends in the West Country.

'Friends — I am no good to them; keep them away from me.'

'But they wish to help you, your grace.'

'Tell them to turn from me while there is yet time to save their own skins.'

It was Devon who eventually persuaded her to take heart and he played upon her emotions by telling her as gently as he could that Henry had once more been taken prisoner and led off to the Tower.

Knowing that she was being blackmailed she consented to the gathering of an army and much against her will agreed to accompany the men as they marched for her.

By the time she reached Bath on the twenty-ninth of April Margaret had an army of considerable size and she was in fairly good hopes of meeting up with Jasper as he came towards her from his strongholds in Wales. Besides the new Duke of Somerset and the Earls of Devon and Oxford she had aroused the sympathy of the countryside and ill-equipped as most of her followers were they seemed united in their intention of restoring Henry to his throne.

It was at Bath where she learnt that Edward had not taken the bait of the few troops she had sent eastward and was making for the west to confront her. Margaret urged her commanders to head for the only bridge over the Severn so that she might join forces with Jasper but at Gloucester they found the town barred.

'My army are so tired that they must rest,' Margaret pleaded with Devon.

'Tired or not, madam, there is nothing for it but to press on; with the Severn bridge closed to us we must be prepared to fight it out.'

Wearily Margaret agreed and the tired and disgruntled men trudged on a further ten miles to seek some kind of rest in the meadows of Tewkesbury. Hardly had they slumped down upon the damp earth and marshy ground close to the river when scouts shouted that Edward and his army were approaching. Bugles sounded and the Lancastrians, hastily pulling on armour and tying rags round their aching and blistered feet, formed into some order on a low hill and prepared to defend themselves.

The sight of the resplendent Edward and his brother, Richard of Gloucester, with their well-accounted army struck dismay into the hearts of those who watched and waited. Margaret's commanders were glad they had persuaded their royal mistress to take shelter with her daughter-in-law in a religious house on the road to Tewkesbury.

The fighting was not prolonged for Edward's superior strength soon broke that of his opponents; he and Richard of Gloucester, their standard bearers at their side, were in the thick of the battle in direct conflict with the Prince of Wales and his supporters. No one was certain who it was that brought about the death of the young son of the Lancastrian queen but by the evening his corpse was joined with that of Devon, John of Somerset and many of the West Country gentry who had flocked to Margaret's banner.

Edward showed no mercy on any who had fought against him and, after a summary court martial, the Duke of Somerset and many other prominent Lancastrians who had been taken prisoner were executed in Tewkesbury.

* * *

Margaret, waiting heavy-hearted with her daughter-in-law and wives of men fighting for her and her son, was brought the news of the disaster by a captain of the guard who crept from the battlefield and hurried her out of her hiding place to a priory somewhere near to Malvern. It was dark by the time she rode into the religious house and she was never certain afterwards where she had been taken. She rode the distance between the two houses in a nightmare of grief and an agony of self-blame.

For two days she lay in a state of shock while nuns with frightened faces tried to get her to take some broth or an opiate to ease her suffering.

On the third morning after the battle the priory was rudely awakened to find a party of Yorkist soldiers banging on the outer door. As a young novice scurried to answer the summons the Abbess heard a man shout: 'Open in the King's name!'

Sir William Stanley followed the troop of military into the yard of the Abbey and demanded that the self-styled queen of the Lancastrians should be brought to him. This message was conveyed to Margaret where she lay in a stupor upon a pallet in a narrow cell.

Speaking almost the first words that she had uttered since she had heard of her son's death she said in a voice so low that the Abbess could hardly understand: 'Tell William Stanley that I am not in the habit of coming to greet mere knights; if he wants me he must come and get me.'

The Abbess conveyed this defiance in some trepidation to Stanley who, fuming backwards and forwards in the white-washed hall of the Abbey, at last agreed to be led into Margaret's room. As he crossed the threshold he unsheathed his sword and stepped up to the bed. Margaret was sitting up now, haggard and red-eyed, propped against the wall.

'There is no need to come against me, a defenceless woman, in arms, Sir William. There is no fight left in me. You have taken my husband and murdered my son. What have you left me?' She stood up and faced him, the once-proud beauty who had captivated a country with her innocence and youth, now a heart-broken woman her countenance ravaged with tears. 'Or perhaps you were given orders to despatch me — if that be the case, let no time be lost for in God's faith I am wearied of this mournful life.'

Moved, despite his animosity for Margaret, Stanley stood aside and gave instructions for his captive to be dressed for a journey and ready to leave within ten minutes.

Turning to Margaret he said: 'The king has left Tewkesbury for a Parliament in Coventry and my instructions are to take you to him to stand trial.'

'The king?' Margaret queried, her mind still numbed with shock. 'Ah, you mean

Edward of York. Let him bring me to the dock but I promise you that there is no further price that he can extort from me for I have paid the penalty of my sins on the field of Tewkesbury.'

Epilogue

It was quiet in the shuttered bedroom of the Chateau Dampierre at Saumur. Margaret lay on her bed and knew that death was not far away. It was August 1482, more than eleven years after that terrible day at Tewkesbury, and part of her had been already dead since then.

All her friends were gone and her father had ended his days in Provence, abandoning her while he lived a life of ease with his wife. Louis had extracted the payment of the debt which he had incurred on her behalf and had claimed the restitution of René's estates to the French crown.

Only Rose and one faithful manservant waited upon her while the three of them eked out an existence on a penurious pension that Louis grudgingly gave.

She was often light-headed during this past summer and in her imagination she held conversations with her son and that gentle husband who had been done to death while she was being dragged, a defeated and monstrous queen, through the streets of London in an open cart like

315

a common whore.

Very occasionally she thought that she was gliding down the Loire beneath the cool trees which shaded its banks while Pierre spoke to her of his undying love and his hopes for the future.

Margaret thought she was dreaming now when she heard, afar off, the tinkling of the outside bell of the chateau and the old manservant's shuffling gait as he went to see who rang. She had almost forgotten the sounds when she heard a voice say: 'Margaret?'

She opened her eyes and in the shadows of the dim, quiet room made out the figure of a man, half-familiar. 'Who is it?' she asked tremulously.

'It is I, Jasper Tudor.'

'Jasper, it cannot be you! How came you here?'

'From Brittany, to present my nephew, Henry Tudor, Earl of Richmond.'

Another form, taller and slimmer, came to stand beside her to take her thin, white hand and kiss it with old-fashioned courtesy. 'My uncle and I heard that you were not well and have come to pay you our respects.' His voice was pleasant, young and firm, overlaid with the Welsh lilt which he had had since his childhood.

'Does Louis know you are here?'

'I do not think so,' Jasper said, with a laugh that stirred the echoes of remembrance. 'His highness of France is still so busy weaving the webs of intrigue that he would not have time to notice a couple of broken-down travellers.'

'Does Francis of Brittany treat you well?'

'He is kind enough,' Henry replied, 'but we come not to speak of ourselves but of you.'

'There is nothing to tell, my life has been a failure — ' Her voice trailed and she was lost to them, dreaming of the days in St. Mihiel.

After a few minutes vigil, Jasper and Henry went quietly out of the room.

'I hope,' Henry said as they went downstairs to eat a meal which Rose was preparing for them, 'that if I am ever given the chance to restore the Lancastrian throne in England I shall prove that far from a failure she was an inspiration to us all.'

'Amen to that,' said Jasper.

317

We do hope that you have enjoyed reading this large print book.

Did you know that all of our titles are available for purchase?

We publish a wide range of high quality large print books including:
Romances, Mysteries, Classics, General Fiction, Non Fiction and Westerns.

Special interest titles available in large print are:
The Little Oxford Dictionary
Music Book
Song Book
Hymn Book
Service Book

Also available from us courtesy of Oxford University Press:
Young Readers' Dictionary
(large print edition)
Young Readers' Thesaurus
(large print edition)

For further information or a free brochure, please contact us at:
Ulverscroft Large Print Books Ltd.,
The Green, Bradgate Road, Anstey,
Leicester, LE7 7FU, England.
Tel: (00 44) **0116 236 4325**
Fax: (00 44) **0116 234 0205**

FIREBALL

Bob Langley

Twenty-seven years ago: the rogue shoot-down of a Soviet spacecraft on a supersecret mission. Now: the SUCHKO 17 suddenly comes back to life three thousand feet beneath the Antarctic ice cap — with terrifying implications for the entire world. The discovery triggers a dark conspiracy that reaches from the depths of the sea to the edge of space — on a satellite with nuclear capabilities. One man and one woman must find the elusive mastermind of a plot with sinister roots in the American military elite, and bring the world back from the edge . . .

STANDING IN THE SHADOWS

Michelle Spring

Laura Principal is repelled but fascinated as she investigates the case of an eleven-year-old boy who has murdered his foster mother. It is not the sort of crime one would expect in Cambridge. The child, Daryll, has confessed to the brutal killing; now his elder brother wants to find out what has turned him into a ruthless killer. Laura confronts an investigation which is increasingly tainted with violence. And that's not all. Someone with an interest in the foster mother's murder is standing in the shadows, watching her every move . . .

NORMANDY SUMMER/ LOVE'S CHARADE

Joy St.Clair

NORMANDY SUMMER — Three cousins, Helen, Tally and Rosie, joined the First Aid Nursing Yeomanry. Helen had driven ambulances through The Blitz, but it was the Summer of 1944 that would change their lives irrevocably.

LOVE'S CHARADE — A broken down car, a mix-up of addresses and soon Kimberley found she was stand-in fianceé for a man she hardly knew. What chance had the pair of them of surviving this masquerade?

THE WESTON WOMEN

Grace Thompson

Wales, 1950s: At the head of the wealthy Weston family are Arfon and Gladys, owners of a once-successful wallpaper and paint store. It had always been Gladys's dream to form a dynasty. Her twin daughters, however, had no interest, and her grandson Jack had little ambition. And so, it is on her twin granddaughters, Joan and Megan, that Gladys pins her hopes. But unbeknown to her, they are considered rather outrageous — and one of them is secretly dating Viv Lewis, who works for the Westons but is not allowed to mix with the family socially. However, it is on him they will depend to help save the business.

TIME AFTER TIME
AND OTHER STORIES

Mary Williams

In this collection of mysterious short stories the recurring theme of 'time after time' is reflected upon with varying intensity, and in several as a haunting reminder of life's immortality. Time itself has little meaning in the wheel of eternity, and it is more than possible that the vital spark or soul of any human being could by chance contact that of another known to him or her in a previous existence on earth. Some stories concentrate on the effect of wandering apparitions about the ether and in all of them can be found love, tragedy, emotional yearnings and sheer terror.